OVERLAND on a SHOESTRING

PETER HURDWELL

Overland on a Shoestring

PETER HURDWELL

Overland on a Shoestring

Copyright © 2013 by Peter Hurdwell.

Paperback ISBN: 978-1-63812-254-8
Ebook ISBN: 978-1-63812-255-5

The views expressed in this work are solely those of the author and do not necessarily reflect the views of the publisher hereby disclaims any responsibility for them.

All rights reserved. No part in this book may be produced and transmitted in any form or by any means, electronic, or mechanical, including photocopying, recording, or by any information storage and retrieval system, without permission in writing from the copyright owner.

Published by Pen Culture Solutions   04/12/2022

Pen Culture Solutions
1-888-727-7204 (USA)
1-800-950-458 (Australia)
support@penculturesolutions.com

Dedication

To my two brothers, Rob and Jerry and to Jerry's wife Lyn, all of whom played prominent roles in planning and participating in the overland journey almost half a century ago.

And also in memory of Jack Warner who sadly died in Sydney in 1992 aged 70 years. His laconic humour was a feature of the overland journey.

Contents

Part 1 | 6
Migration From Post War, Britain,
The Ten Pound Tourist, Return To Britain
The Seeds Are Sown.

Part 2 | 11
Planning And Preparation, The Dummy Run, Final Touches.

Part 3 | 17
Leaving England, Norway, Sweden, Denmark.

Part 4 | 23
Europe
Germany, Switzerland, Italy, Greece, Turkey

Part 5 | 34
Asia
Turkey, Iran, West Pakistan, India, Himalyas, Nepal, East Pakistan,
Burma, Thailand, Singapore

Part 6 | 76
Australia

Part One

AUSTRALIA

Overland On A Shoestring

Migration from Post War Britain - The Ten Pound Tourist - Return to Britain - The Seed is Sown

MIGRATION **FROM** POST WAR BRITAIN - 1959.

After the Second World War, Britain had become a vastly different country from that which had existed in 1939. How could it not have been so?

The war had seen the German bombing of a large number of the heavily populated industrial centres on the Island Nation and many of its inhabitants had endured the horrors of war first hand.

Thousands of children from those heavily populated towns had been evacuated to the relative safety of country villages, to be cared for by people whom they had never met and in an environment quite foreign to them. Many of them were not only separated from their mothers but some had experienced the additional hardship of not seeing their fathers for months, if not years due to their conscription into the British forces. Many of these fathers never lived to return to their families in Britain.

With so many changes experienced in their early lives, many children from that generation developed a sense of adventure and individuality at a tender age and were more adaptable to change than their forbears. A large number had developed minds that were less circumscribed than their antecedents which enabled them to cast their fates to the winds of change blowing through the world following the end of hostilities.

Having completed their formal education these young people left school and joined the permanent workforce only to find that the British class system, whilst having been somewhat ameliorated by the war years, was nevertheless little diminished from the pre-war years. A youth hailing from the privileged classes and armed with the twin advantages of socially acceptable parentage and an education at a prestigious public school would be more likely to be propelled into the upper echelons of the business world than would his or her grammar school counterpart.

Thus, for some younger British citizens their aspirations sometimes led them to thoughts of seeking a new life in a foreign land where the possibilities of more fertile opportunities beckoned.

Britain also faced the monumental task of rebuilding its cities and infrastructure after the war in addition to the challenge of paying off the massive debt that it had amassed in order to finance its war effort. For the average individual money was tight and people in Britain faced the prospect of lean times well into the foreseeable future.

On the other hand, underpopulated young countries within the British Empire were at that time crying out for new settlers to swell their ranks in order to expand their development. They were particularly interested in recruiting well educated young migrants with preference being given to those whose native tongue was English.

Australia was at the forefront of this immigration push. During the Second World War Australia's very existence had been threatened by imminent invasion by the Imperial Japanese Army and Darwin had been the subject of months of Japanese bombing, not to mention a submarine raid in Sydney Harbour. Australia felt that in order to protect itself against future military aggression it needed a larger population and to address this need it centred its focus on Europe and especially Great Britain.

As a consequence Australia instituted an immigration policy designed to attract new migrants to its shores.

Its advertising campaigns in Britain often featured a bronzed Adonis with rippling muscles plunging into foaming surf or nubile young women with curvaceous breasts pointing heavenward against the backdrop of cloudless blue skies as they lay in skimpy swimsuits on the golden sands of an Australian beach. The Australian government offered prospective migrants these sumptuous prospects plus a cruise on an ocean liner into the bargain for the minuscule sum of ten British pounds, the only stipulation being that the migrant would be obliged to stay for a minimum of two years. Those who accepted the offer were known as 'ten pound tourists' or 'ten pound Poms'.

Little wonder that younger people from Britain sought the opportunity for adventure of travelling to a distant land with a built-in option of returning to Britain after two years if they chose to go back. Many young people, particularly those with a trade, availed themselves of this offer of a new life in another country where the prospect of higher pay was almost assured whilst others pictured themselves luxuriating in sunny climes without the unfriendly promise of icy blasts so typical of Northern European winters.

Inevitably descriptions of life from satisfied migrants in the new world filtered back to friends in the old country and whetted the appetites of those who had been toying with the notion of a life other than in Britain.

It is against this backdrop that one young man at the age of twenty-six decided to become a 'ten pound tourist'.

THE TEN POUND TOURIST

My elder brother Jerry was five years old and I was two when the Second World War commenced in September, 1939. Although the London suburb in which we lived with our parents was outwardly unaffected during the first few months of the war it suffered severe effects from enemy bombing from 1940 onwards, firstly by the Luftwaffe and in the final year of the war through damage by V 1 Flying Bombs and latterly the V 2 Long Range Rockets, both of which caused enormous devastation.

In 1940 it was decided by our parents that Jerry and I together with our mother should be evacuated to the relative safety of a small country village to the south of Camberley in southern England. Our year long stay was not a happy one as the local folk seemed to resent our presence and made us feel rather unwelcome, especially the children who were somewhat unfriendly to my brother who by then was attending the local school.

It was therefore decided that we should return to London as our mother felt that it was less demoralising to endure the German bombing than the hostility of the local village populace. It also meant that we would be able to rejoin our Dad who was employed as a London policeman. Thus we returned to London in 1942 and survived the rest of the war although over a hundred inhabitants in our suburb lost their lives during German air raids, in fact the very first V 2 Rocket ever sent to Britain landed only a kilometre from our home.

At the conclusion of the war, Jerry had attended almost a dozen schools including the local school in Chingford where lessons had been curtailed after sustaining extensive damage during an air raid. By the time he left school at the age of fifteen his education had resembled a patchwork quilt but without the common thread required to have woven it into a useful education. Thus, upon starting work at the office of a printing company in January, 1950, he attended evening classes for three years in order to catch up on the education which had unfortunately been denied him during the war years.

Although peace was restored in 1945 Britain introduced National Service whereby male youths were conscripted into the armed forces at the age of eighteen and were obliged to serve for two years in uniform, often being posted overseas. Jerry was therefore called up into the British Army in 1952 and served in the Suez Canal Zone in Egypt, being demobilized two years later.

After two years National Service he found it very difficult to settle down to a hum drum office job back in London. At that time Canada and Australia were seeking migrants and he was initially attracted to migrating to Canada where he had a friend in Vancouver. He mentioned this to his close friend who liked the idea of emigrating but said "If you are contemplating a warm place like Australia I'll come with you".

After agreeing to migrate to Australia together they underwent interviews and medical examinations at Australia House in London and were given a sailing date for May, 1960. However, shortly before they were due to embark, his friend succumbed to the charms of an attractive young lady and decided to stay in England to marry her. Disappointed but not deterred Jerry decided to set off on his own as a guest of Her Majesty's Government of Australia.

In May, 1960 he made his way to Tilbury Docks where he boarded RMS Orion, a 23,000 ton steam turbine vessel built in 1935 which had recently been fitted out for the sole purpose of transporting European migrants to Australia.

The beginning of his journey was not without its mishaps as he had left his hand luggage on the bed at home and had departed for the docks without it, only to be found by my younger brother Rob and our father after returning from a morning's tennis. Still in sweaty tennis gear they drove the thirty kilometres to Tilbury Docks and just managed to hand over Jerry's chattels moments before he boarded the ship.

He certainly enjoyed the trip noting that the accommodation on the 'RMS Orion' was luxurious and in stark contrast to the troop ship 'SS Empire Ken' that had conveyed him to Egypt several years before where he had been posted in the British Army.

Eventually the vessel arrived in Australian waters and docked at Fremantle, Adelaide and then Melbourne before sailing on to Sydney. Approaching 'The Heads' at Sydney the ship was met by a Pilot vessel that also deposited a supply of Sydney Morning Herald newspapers on the 'Orion' which continued steaming along the shores of the harbour, under the Harbour Bridge, eventually mooring at Number Thirteen Wharf, Pyrmont. (Fortunately he was not a superstitious person).

Armed with a copy of Friday's Sydney Morning Herald, Jerry scanned the 'positions vacant' columns and chanced upon an advertisement for a job at the 'Albion Insurance Company' in the Central Business District of the city and duly applied for an interview using a ship-to-shore telephone on the 'Orion'.

Once on shore he went through the normal immigration formalities and boarded an ancient green and cream Government bus which had seen better days several decades before. It transported him to a migrant hostel in Rooty Hill, a somewhat less than salubrious suburb in those days and situated about forty kilometres west of the centre of Sydney. The facilities at the hostel were very basic and consisted of old Nissen huts left over after the Second World War and uncomfortable enough to persuade him that his first priority was to find alternative accommodation. However, for him to achieve this would first require his having a permanent job.

It was not uncommon for offices in Sydney to open for business on Saturday mornings so he donned his suit and made his way to the offices of the Albion Insurance Company in George Street, Sydney where he was interviewed by the General Manager, Mr Noel Evans.

After working in the stiff and starchy atmosphere of a Lloyds insurance broking house in the City of London the culture shock of the Sydney office soon became apparent. Upon addressing the Manager as 'Sir' he was unceremoniously told that "Holy Ghost mate, my name's Noel!" Most culture shocks tend to be quite daunting but the company's newest prospective employee immediately felt at home in the relaxed atmosphere.

He was offered a position as a fire and accident clerk with the Albion and having agreed to start work the following Tuesday he set about finding accommodation. Like most English people the only place in Sydney that he had ever heard of was Bondi Beach so an estate agency provided him with a few addresses in Bondi. He settled on the first flat he inspected in Gould Street, not far from the beach. It was a small single room with shared bathroom /toilet but the rent had been discounted due to the previous tenant having committed suicide in the room. The rent was two pounds fifteen shillings per week.

His next task was to return to the migrant hostel at Rooty Hill, to collect his baggage and transport it to his newly acquired flat in Bondi.

Although he had passed his driving test only a month before leaving England he hired a Ute (utility truck) from a car yard at Kings Cross in Sydney and somehow found his way back to Rooty Hill where he collected his chattels and was installed in his new flat by midnight.

Three days after landing in Sydney he had secured a job and a flat and unbeknown to him at the time, was shortly to meet his future wife. He soon came to the realisation that with a bit of energy and initiative things could certainly move at a brisk pace in the new world in which he found himself.

On his first day at work the ten pound tourist was a little nervous as he entered the building in which the Albion Insurance Company transacted its business. Dressed in his clerical grey pinstripe suit and wearing a white shirt with a shiny starched detachable collar, he must have looked rather odd compared with the other male members of the staff. However, it took very little time for him to warm to the relaxed and informal atmosphere of the office and he was very well accepted by other members of the staff, particularly Lyn, the manager's secretary, a tall, trim attractive blonde.

When he asked the General Manager which member of staff would be able to do his typing, Noel Evans said "Take Lyn, Jerry" He took the invitation quite literally and it appears that the attraction must have been mutual as they started going out together. After Jerry had purchased a new Renault Dauphine car he was able to drive out to Cronulla, a southern suburb of Sydney, to spend weekends with Lyn and her family.

They eventually married in September, 1962 and two months later boarded the 'RMS Arcadia' for a journey to England where Lyn was to meet the Hurdwell family for the first time. Their stay was to last for a period of two years before their return to Australia.

Little could they have imagined at the time that their return journey to Australia would not be aboard a ship nor on an aircraft - it would be overland through Europe and Asia - and they would not be alone.

RETURN TO BRITAIN

Their landing at Tilbury Docks happened to coincide with one of the most severe winters Britain had ever experienced, when the ice on the River Thames became so thick that even heavy trucks were able to drive on it. There were heavy falls of snow, icy roads and the most of the houses were bitterly cold as central heating was a luxury that only the wealthy were able to afford.

Although we all enjoyed sliding on the icy lakes or careering down makeshift toboggan runs, nothing could disguise the fact that we were almost always miserably cold.

Lyn was not only frozen to the marrow most of the time but was also homesick for the sun drenched beaches she had left behind. However, as they both intended to stay in England for only two years they decided to make the most of it and enjoyed all the wonders which Britain had to offer particularly after the icy weather had given way to spring and summer.

OVERLAND - THE SEED IS SOWN

Whilst returning to live in Australia was never far from their minds, they had always assumed that the homeward journey would be by ocean liner, such journeys offering a relaxing holiday with the cost being substantially lower than air travel at that time.

However, in early 1963 five friends were enjoying a drink at 'The Green Dragon' pub in Waltham Abbey, Essex when the subject of Jerry and Lyn's returning to Australia was mentioned. Geoff Kirk who had recently finished his accountancy examinations, was enthusiastic about the idea of living in Australia when my brothers Jerry and Rob first mentioned the subject of an overland trip. Lyn was certainly interested in the idea as was Anne, Geoff's young wife. At that stage the idea was a mere skeleton and it was to take several months before fleshing into a feasible project.

One member of the group had recently read the account of a journey from Britain to Singapore overland that had been undertaken five years earlier although that group had been fortunate enough to have been sponsored by a variety of different companies including the use of two new Land Rovers.

Geoff and Anne had been contemplating moving to Sydney for some time as Geoff had been offered a job there by his accountancy firm in London that had offices in Sydney. He also told the group that he had a friend, Brian Birrell, who had just completed his studies as a dentist and who might also be interested in such a venture.

My younger brother Rob, who worked for a timber company in London, had also been contemplating a trip to Australia but had no plans to settle there, preferring to merely have a look at the country and broaden his horizons.

Amongst our circle of friends word got around and a friend with whom Jerry and I had once worked said that he was also interested in the journey. Jack Warner was quite a bit older than the rest of us, having spent the war years as Chief Petty Officer on the British aircraft carrier 'HMS Victorious'.

As preliminary discussions about the trip took place at our parents' house in Chingford, I too became interested in the overland trip which presented itself as the opportunity of a lifetime and a chance to see things I had only ever read about in magazines and history books.

Thus, the participants in the undertaking were

Jerry and Lyn Hurdwell

Geoff and Anne Kirk

Rob and Pete Hurdwell

Brian Birrell

Jack Warner

Part Two
Planning & Preparation
The Dummy Run - Final Touches

PLANNING AND PREPARATION

We were under no illusions as to how difficult it would be to prepare for a trip that was to cover thousands of kilometres on roads and remote tracks and would also cross a large number of sovereign borders, with some countries having been or with the prospect of being politically unstable.

Having decided on an approximate date for our departure many items came up for discussion, not least of which was the route to be taken through Europe and Asia before arriving in Australia. The route to be taken would also have a considerable bearing on the types of vehicles to be used.

It was therefore decided that instead of setting foot on the European Continent at Calais via the British port of Dover, we would drive north to Newcastle in England and ferry the vehicles across the North Sea to Bergen in Norway. Except for myself, none of the other participants had ever been to Scandinavia and my only experience had been a couple of weeks in Denmark on a NATO military exercise during my service in Germany as a conscripted soldier in the British Army six years before.

We planned to land in Bergen, Norway and then motor south to Sweden, Denmark, Germany, Switzerland, Italy, Greece, Turkey, Iran, West Pakistan, India, Nepal, East Pakistan (now Bangladesh) Burma, Thailand, Malaysia, Singapore and thence by air to Australia, hopefully arriving in Sydney before Christmas 1964 after approximately six months from the commencement of our journey.

Having mapped out our proposed route and researched conditions likely to be experienced en route we decided that four wheel drive vehicles would be essential, particularly for the six thousand or so kilometres involving rough sandy desert roads in Turkey, Iran and West Pakistan.

Unlike that British expedition of a few years before, we could not expect to be given the use of new Land Rovers and our finances were very limited indeed. It was therefore suggested that we should obtain three ex army World War II American Willy's Jeeps.

It took us a few weeks but we finally managed to track down three such vehicles. Jerry, Rob and Lyn in one, Geoff, Anne and Brian in another with Jack and myself in the third vehicle, each party being responsible for the overhaul and maintenance of their own vehicle. However, once the trip was under way Geoff, Jack and I would be primarily responsible for the repair and maintenance of the vehicles.

Geoff was an excellent motor mechanic having built his own open sports car from parts off an old 1935 Austin Seven Swallow Special saloon car, whilst Jack and I possessed quite a lot of experience in motor vehicle repairs and maintenance. The Jeep that Jack and I had purchased for seventy guineas (just over seventy-three pounds) looked to be in quite good condition but having driven it to Jack's home in Sutton, Surrey we found that a lot of work would still be required before the overland journey was to be undertaken.

The three speed gearbox was very sloppy, particularly second gear which tended to drop into neutral unless held in place. The engine had a rather unhealthy propensity to burn oil so we decided to either fit oversize piston rings or have the cylinders rebored. However, after stripping the engine down, we found that the cylinder bores were already sixty thousandths of an inch oversize suggesting that they had been rebored three times already.

However after several months of work in bitterly cold winter conditions which numbed our hands and made working for long periods impossible, we managed to get our own 1942 ex US Army Jeep into reasonable shape. Our work included decarbonising the four cylinders and lapping in new engine valves, removing the transfer and main gearboxes which we reconditioned. Jack also built an aluminium body with pin-back doors that we fitted to the chassis. Brakes were relined and completely reconditioned.

The hand brake was an odd contraption as it worked off the propeller shaft with a calliper pressing down onto the brake lining situated on the drive shaft just behind the gearbox. Although we had rebuilt the gearbox and fitted a new oil seal, the oil still managed to seep out onto the brake lining. However, by securing a metal cocoa tin onto the propeller shaft behind the gearbox we were able to overcome the problem by diverting the errant oil away from the hand brake lining.

Having researched weather conditions likely to be encountered on the journey we predicted that in many countries, particularly the Iranian desert, temperatures would be extremely high and there would be every chance that re-starting the vehicles during the fierce heat of the day could be difficult. It was more than likely that petrol would evaporate before reaching the cylinders thus inhibiting combustion of the petrol. However, I managed to find a motor vehicle breakers' yard where they had a clapped out 1936 Morris 8 car that possessed a six volt electric fuel pump. We fitted this pump in series with the existing cam driven pump and felt that the extra boost in petrol whilst re-starting a hot engine should overcome such problems, particularly in high temperatures likely to be experienced under desert conditions.

It had originally been our intention to sell the vehicles in Malaysia or Singapore at the end of the land journey but we found that we would have to pay a hefty amount of money by way of a bond that specifically precluded us from selling the vehicles in all countries en route to Singapore. However after much research we were able to ascertain that we might be able to sell the vehicles in Nepal and still be able to redeem our bonds. It therefore followed that we had little alternative but to end our motoring journey in Kathmandu and find alternative means of local transport thereafter.

Meanwhile Geoff was making considerable progress in overhauling the second Jeep on his own. As Brian Birrell lived a considerable distance away in Newport Pagnell, it had proven impracticable for him to travel to Geoff's home on a regular basis. Also, it is highly unlikely that motor vehicle mechanical repairs would have claimed any prominence on his curriculum vitae.

Alas, news of the last Jeep was not so good. Jerry and Rob had rented a garage nearby in which they were keeping the Jeep but with the onset of winter and the bitterly cold weather, tragedy struck. Upon starting the engine one morning they noticed that after a while water started to seep from engine block. We suspected that the below zero temperatures had popped out a welch plug but further scrutiny confirmed our worst fears – the engine block had cracked.

Various enquiries were made as to how to fix the problem, one possible remedy being to have the engine block 'stitch welded'. However, as our proposed journey would involve extremes of temperatures, ranging from the nights on the fringe of the Arctic Circle to days in the heat of the Iranian Desert, it was decided that we could not take the risk. Thus, not long after acquiring the vehicle it was disposed of.

Scanning a copy of the 'Exchange and Mart' trading magazine Jerry and Rob came across a 1955 1500cc Bedford CAV Van for the princely sum of fifty British pounds. After inspecting the vehicle and taking it for a run they paid the money and drove it home.

The owners of the two remaining Jeeps were a little concerned that the new acquisition would not be suited to the expected terrain and conditions, particularly when driving through desert sands. However, our apprehensions were somewhat mollified by thoughts that should the Bedford be stuck in a sand drift there were a couple of four-wheel-drive vehicles on hand to pull it out. Also, the Bedford would be able to carry more stores than the cramped Jeeps and had the advantage of being thirteen years their junior.

Once the Bedford had been garaged we had a chance to inspect it in more detail and found it to be in quite good condition. The clutch showed little signs of wear and the brake drums and linings did not require replacement. Although there was a little bit of play in the timing chain it did not at the time appear to require attention. The only money they had to spend on the vehicle was for five retreaded tyres costing four pounds each and two jerry cans. Prior to the trip the jerry cans were to be filled with aviation fuel that would be used to boost the vehicle's performance when negotiating the difficult mountain road up to Kathmandu. When they eventually sold the vehicle they filled the tank with this 'rocket fuel' and the new owner was most impressed with the power output of such a small engine. Fortunately Jerry and Rob were gone by the time the vehicle was reintroduced to its normal diet of eighty octane petrol.

In order to take advantage of the extra space provided by the van, Jerry and Rob installed storage shelves and also rigged up a removable shelf on the side of the vehicle to enable food and beverages to be prepared more conveniently.

Similar facilities were provided for the Jeeps by making table tops that could be rested upon the front bumper bars with two collapsible legs at the other end to add stability. Each vehicle was equipped with a tool kit, puncture outfit complete with hand pump and a spade to be used for excavating latrines, drainage trenches and also for digging vehicles out of mud or sand.

Due to the age of the vehicles a great deal of thought was given as to what spare parts should be carried bearing in mind that we had limited storage space and limited funds as well. However we

decided to err on the side of caution and managed to stock a reasonably comprehensive supply of parts for the vehicles whose reliability was likely to be at risk given the conditions we were contemplating. Among these items were spares such as petrol pump repair kits, cylinder valves and valve grinding paste, spark plugs, spare distributor parts, fan belts, brake linings, fuel lines, a soldering iron and solder plus various sizes of nuts and bolts. Large and heavy items such as vehicle batteries were deemed not to have been essential as it was reasonable to expect that such generic items would be available en route.

Having been in contact with the Institute for Tropical Medicines in London we were given a list of the vaccinations that would be required for the countries we were visiting. Having obtained these, our general practitioners administered all but the yellow fever injections. For these we had to attend the Institute for Tropical Medicine which provided and administered the required jabs.

It was assumed that during the journey multifarious stomach bugs and bacteria would invade our intestines, so Brian was charged with the task of researching possible health hazards and also the means of diagnosing and giving relief and cures when they occurred. He even researched how, in an emergency, he would be able to carry out an appendectomy although we were all terrified should such a necessity arise. It appeared to us that the comparison between pulling a tooth and excising an appendix was a bridge too far and a circumstance too grisly to even contemplate.

We planned to carry as much tinned and dried food as possible although for the first few thousand kilometres we would be able to eat the local food. Fresh fruit and vegetables would be in abundant supply in Europe during the northern summer. Doubtless the variety of fresh foods would diminish and quality would deteriorate the further our trip progressed. We budgeted six shillings and eight pence per person per day for the purchase of food during the journey

Rob spent some considerable time researching what maps would be required. Although we had a general idea of the proposed route, maps that gave specific details were not readily available. In 1963 there were of course no computers or the internet to speed up the research process and to provide vital information. He therefore had to rely on writing letters and making phone calls in order to carry out this most important task. A wrong turn in the midst of some remote wilderness could be fraught with problems and danger.

Geoff's knowledge as an accountant proved to be invaluable and he was able to arrange for us to draw money from local banks en route rather than taking travellers' cheques which posed the ever present problem of theft or loss. He was also able to work out how much we needed to budget for food, accommodation, housekeeping, petrol and other necessities.

Almost fifty years ago camping and the means of cooking meals in the open air were almost prehistoric compared with facilities in the twenty-first century. Portable gas and kerosene stoves were considered not to have been an option for us. As petrol was the fuel required to power the vehicles, we purchased several collapsible petrol fired stoves.

Back in those days tents with sewn-in groundsheets did not exist and the fabrics with which tents were made were cumbersome and required the application of liquid water repellents to keep out the rain. We therefore required tents that could accommodate two or three occupants but that

were simple to erect, were waterproof and sturdy enough to withstand many weeks of continuous use. We therefore purchased three tents of different sizes, two of which required poles and fly sheets with the third relying on a pneumatic frame in place of poles. Jerry and Rob already owned the 'igloo' style tent which was erected by pumping up the conical frame with the use of a motor vehicle hand pump. Once up it afforded the maximum amount of space without the encroachments of centre poles. Each of the tents required separate ground sheets.

Each of us possessed two separate sleeping bags, one lightweight and one designed for colder weather. We predicted that for most of the journey we would need only the lighter bag but as the desert areas were known for their extremes in temperature we would require the use of two bags to cope with the bitterly cold nights. Inflatable 'Lilo' mattresses were also purchased as they were able to provide maximum amount of comfort without taking up too much valuable storage space.

As mosquitoes and other bugs were going to be a continual hazard we each acquired a mosquito net and predicted that from Southern Europe onwards we would be able to sleep under the stars in our sleeping bags, protected by the nets.

THE DUMMY RUN

After many months of preparation and second guessing problems which were likely to arise we decided to hold a weekend 'dummy run' and chose Hastings in the south of England as the venue. Looking back it seems strange to endeavour to simulate a journey to the other side of the globe with a hundred and fifty kilometre trip to Hastings where, ironically Harold, King of England was killed in 1066.

The weekend was hardly a template for the real thing. It rained constantly and the only element of excitement was an experience at a pub on the journey down. We were sitting in the pub enjoying a beer when a large German shepherd dog pushed the swing doors open, made his way to our table and started snarling at Jerry. Unfortunately, at that time nobody in our party had been designated as Security Officer but Rob decided to take on the mantel and elected himself ad hoc to the position. Grabbing an upturned chair he managed to push the dog backwards like a circus lion trainer until it was finally ejected from the pub, much to the applause of the assembled company. Following this altercation we discussed the specific duties of the participants. The talents or lack thereof of the party were assessed and taken into account, resulting in the following responsibilities being assigned.

GEOFF	Finance & Mechanic	JERRY	General Dogsbody
ROB	Navigator	JACK	Security
BRIAN	Medical	ANNE	Food & Provisions
PETE	Mechanic	LYN	Diet & Provisions

We eventually arrived at Hastings and spent a little while finding a wooded area which, as it had no facilities was therefore more likely to represent at least to a certain degree the type of location we were to experience on the first part of the journey. Setting up our tents and field kitchen it soon became apparent that the area was infested by annoying mosquitoes and I soon became the victim of their activities. However, it did give us a chance to put the mosquito nets to good use as we were able to seek sanctuary under them inside our tents.

Upon returning home the following Sunday afternoon it was agreed that although we really hadn't learned much during the dummy run we did manage to have some fun and had also found a great pub in Hastings into the bargain.

FINAL TOUCHES

A week before the journey was due to commence we got together for the last time at our parents' home. Our parents were obviously concerned about their three sons undertaking the journey especially as Jerry and Lyn were planning to live permanently in Australia. At that time cheap air fares were not even on the horizon and a return flight from Sydney to London would cost as much as a year's wages, with the journey taking three days.

However, Rob and I had planned to return to England after saving enough money for the return journey by sea. Nevertheless, I think that our mother who was a most perceptive and intuitive person, suspected that knowing our personalities and the easy-going informality of the Australian lifestyle, we would find it difficult to tear ourselves away and return to the somewhat more stolid existence which England offered at that time.

Part Three
Leaving England
Norway - Sweden - Denmark

LEAVING ENGLAND

First Day - 29th June, 1964

We woke up at dawn just as the sun was peeping over the horizon, not that we could actually see the horizon as we were living in a populous London suburb. However, we knew that as our journey progressed we would come to welcome the dawn in almost total isolation whether it be the rugged fjords of Scandinavia or the desolate deserts of the Middle East.

But today was the first step towards such experiences and we were embarking upon what we imagined would be the journey of a lifetime. Our trip would take us overland for thousands of kilometres through nineteen different countries and take five or six months to complete.

Although we were excited about the forthcoming journey it was naturally tinged with sadness. Our mother was very upset to see her three sons leaving home all at the same time. She left the house as we were still making last minute preparations to load up the vehicles. She sat outside in the family Mini whilst our father came into the house, shook hands with each one of us and walked out to his car. Our mother never looked back as she and Dad drove off.

We eventually left Chingford at 11.40 am and called at a Willy's Jeep spare parts dealership in Hampstead for last minute spares that we thought might be needed en route. Having done this we headed north to Newport Pagnell where Brian Birrell was living with his parents.

Not far from Brian's home the journey for our Jeep (registration prefix LVW) was almost ended when a Morris Minor car unexpectedly and without warning pulled out of a small side street in front of us causing our vehicle to swerve violently all over the road, in fact for a moment our heavily laden Jeep actually balanced on only two wheels before managing to right itself.

Having enjoyed a sumptuous meal with Brian's parents and his fiancée, Brian hopped aboard Geoff's Jeep (registration prefix RYF) and we were finally on our way north along the A1 trunk road. Fifteen kilometres south of Newark we camped in a field. We were all in good humour but could hardly believe that we were actually on our way. Having nibbled a mere couple of hundred kilometres off a journey of over twenty thousand kilometres, Australia seemed to be a very long way away.

The following day we continued motoring north but lost sight of Jeep RYF somewhere around Doncaster but managed to regroup later, eventually camping next to a rubbish dump, two miles the other side of Durham. In the evening we enjoyed the luxury of our last drink in the UK at a delightful pub and later took the opportunity of looking around picturesque scenery along the river.

In bright July sunshine the following day we hit the road early to enable us to meet up with Geoff's parents at Gateshead where they had prepared an enormous meal. Even just a few days in the fresh air had ensured that we would possess excellent appetites and we did justice to the food set before us thinking that any reserves stored up now would be invaluable further down the track.

We were surprised to find that the local inhabitants had not only heard of our impending journey but displayed a great deal of interest in it, in fact a reporter from one of the local newspapers arrived on the scene seeking information for an article.

Having bid farewell to Geoff's parents we were happy to climb into our Jeeps and Bedford van, pin the doors back and enjoy the sunny weather as we drove over the Tyne Bridge that links Gateshead and Newcastle. The significance of the Tyne Bridge was not lost on us as it had been built by Dorman Long, its construction having been completed in 1928. At three hundred and eighty-nine metres long it had been a great improvement on the previous stone bridge but was small by comparison to the Sydney Harbour Bridge also built by Dorman Long from the same design four years later.

When we saw the Sydney Harbour Bridge for the first time nearly seven months later, the similarity was obvious. Driving over it we learned to appreciate that whereas the Newcastle Bridge was less than four hundred metres long, its colonial sister was a massive one and a quarter kilometres in length and wide enough to accommodate eight lanes of motor traffic, a pedestrian footway, two railways tracks and a cycleway.

Eventually we arrived at the Bergen Line Ferry Terminal where we boarded, of all things, the good ship Venus at 3.30 pm. As it wasn't a 'drive-on-drive-off' ferry the vehicles had to be loaded onto the vessel by means of a derrick. Loading was a breathtaking experience as we wondered whether the old Bedford would fold up under the strain.

Our voyage on the SS Venus had been underway for only a very short time when we encountered very heavy seas, so heavy in fact that all passengers were required to remain below decks. However, after a night's sleep followed by breakfast we were allowed on deck, eventually berthing at Bergen at 4.00 pm the following day local time where we were welcomed by torrential rain.

SCANDINAVIA
NORWAY

Having driven a few miles north of the harbour city we camped in a meadow. The weather conditions were extremely unpleasant to the point where our clothes were soaking wet, but notwithstanding this we went for a long walk, returning to camp two hours later to boil the billy and retire to bed at midnight. Being so far north of the equator it was still daylight.

Although the torrential rain continued throughout the following day we decided to drive back into Bergen itself where we visited the markets for fresh supplies. As Bergen is a sea port and market town we purchased some fresh fish for our evening meal before driving on, still in the pouring rain and on atrocious roads to Oystese where we intended to stay at the local Youth Hostel.

We managed to gain some respite from the foul weather when we drove through a long tunnel, however the headlights on the LVW Jeep failed and all but blotted out our visibility. As Jack was driving I managed to find my torch and pointed it forward by leaning out of the open door although this was indeed a very unpleasant experience.

By the next morning the rain clouds had disappeared and the sun was shining, lifting our spirits considerably. What a tonic this was considering that the last time we had seen sunshine had been in England, not normally renowned for its sunny weather. Having swept out the hostel and cleaned the dishes we took advantage of the better weather to take a walk around Oystese and up into the surrounding countryside. The hills were dotted with waterfalls feeding rivers which eventually flowed into the lakes below whilst on the horizon some of the mountains were still capped with last winter's snow even though we were now approaching mid-summer.

After a bowl of freshly made soup and local bread we drove to the ferry which conveyed our party to Eidfjord. Once again the scenery was spectacular with rugged peaks capped with snow. It was at Eidfjord that we camped on the banks of the fjord without any sign of habitation as far as the eye could see.

We were on the road early the next morning as we intended to arrive at Gol, our next destination before evening. The road we took was really only a dusty, pebbled track interspersed with a number of hairpin bends. Fortunately we encountered no other traffic throughout the day in either direction. As our vehicles chugged up the many hills the temperature became noticeably cooler to the point where halfway into our journey we stepped out of the vehicles and enjoyed snowball fights and sliding down the snowy slopes on our backsides. This enjoyable diversion was curtailed when the cold weather prompted us to return to our vehicles and place our sodden buttocks on the seats, an experience which was rather unpleasant.

We eventually set up camp in the early evening only a kilometre or so the other side of Gol and having lit a camp fire we luxuriated in its warmth, thawing out our hands and drying out our steaming clothing.

As we had planned to do some sightseeing in Oslo the next day, we selected a campsite that had previously been recommended, situated on the outskirts of that city, but had trouble in locating it. However, having finally located it we found that it was not what we had been expecting. Instead of being quiet and well laid out we were dismayed to see that it was populated by a throng of noisy holiday makers frantically dashing around in an effort to enjoy themselves. It resembled the less attractive dual aspects of both a regimental training depot and a Butlin's holiday camp. As it was too late in the day to move on, we had no choice but to erect our tents and make the best of it. We had driven south for several hundred kilometres and had been expecting warmer weather but were surprised to notice that in the morning there was nevertheless a thin dusting of frost on the ground.

Dressed in what for us were the best clothes we could muster we drove into Oslo the following day and visited some very well laid out parks noticing that the Norwegians seemed to have been very keen on nude statues in fact everywhere we looked there were statues of men, women and even children of all shapes and sizes engaged in various activities, but all stark naked.

However the highlight of our visit in Oslo was to a museum complex housing various exhibits including the Kon Tiki Museum. As an eleven year old boy at high school I had avidly read Thor Heyerdahl's book 'Kon Tiki Expedition' and had been captivated by the crew's adventure, even

picturing myself spending a hundred and one days on a balsa raft as it sailed four thousand three hundred kilometres on its journey from South America to Polynesia. However when confronted by the raft in the museum I was amazed at its size. It was far larger than I had ever imagined.

We also visited the Viking Museum where original Viking ships were on display. It seemed strange that the occupants of these wonderfully constructed vessels could have travelled for such long distances through treacherous seas, making a huge impact on the east coast of Great Britain. It is well within the realms of possibility that some of our party might have inherited Viking blood.

Within the same complex was the 'Fram' Museum but at the time of our visit I had not been aware of the significance of Roald Amundsen's vessel that had conveyed the explorer and his men to the Antarctic as a precursor to their successful assault on the South Pole.

It was significant that the vessel was powered by a petrol engine, an unusual innovation for Antarctic journeys at that time. As history was to relate, Amundsen and his party reached the South Pole on 14th December, 1911 which incidentally was the day our mother would have been celebrating her first birthday. Alas, for Robert Falcon Scott's party they arrived at the Pole five weeks later only to find a tent left by Amundsen. Disappointed and downhearted Scott and his party perished on the return journey to Scott Base. Visiting this museum was an opportunity missed although one day I hope to rectify that omission.

Returning to the camping ground we were fortunate enough to just make it to bed before the heavens opened yet again and another storm broke, drenching our encampment. It pelted down all night, giving us an excuse to remain in bed a while longer rather than face the elements. During a brief break in the weather we struck camp, loaded the sodden camping gear into the vehicles and motored south towards Sweden, eventually setting up camp about eighty kilometres from the Swedish border. Although the site we had selected was situated next to a road and a railway line there was a barn nearby which, as it transpired, became a definite plus for our party. During the night when another storm came up making life in the tents very uncomfortable, a number of our party took shelter in the barn.

Next morning we got up a lot earlier than usual, vacating the area before 9 am without encountering the owner before we left.

Knowing that food in Sweden would be expensive we decided to purchase items of food in Norway prior to crossing the border.

SWEDEN

Crossing into Sweden was quite interesting as we were required to proceed through a short tunnel driving on the right hand side of the road before emerging in Sweden having switched to the left. In 1964 the Swedes drove on the same side as the British. It was several years later that Sweden joined their Scandinavian and Continental cousins in driving on the right.

Once in Sweden we purchased a few items of food and noted that the costs were astronomical by comparison to Norway. We found Swedish towns and villages to be very clean and tidy, pervading an air of sanitised opulence wherever we went. This may have been a reflection upon Sweden having remained neutral during two world wars.

We experienced one small mishap in Sweden when the Bedford became bogged in a ditch and had to be towed out by one of the Jeeps. However we all arrived safely at the very expensive campsite where we spent the night.

On the morning of 10th July we woke up to beautiful sunshine which was a great relief particularly as the rain had been bucketing down onto our tents throughout the night. Our spirits rose as we drove to Gothenburg for a look around. We must have looked somewhat out of place dressed in our well worn but practical travelling attire by comparison to the well dressed local men and chic, attractive young blonde women.

Returning to our vehicles we joined the local rush hour traffic out of town until reaching a more rural area where we were able to find a suitable camping spot a long way from the city. Enjoying the warm evening we sat around feeling relieved to be out of the rush and bustle of the city. As we were chatting some Swedish youths aged no more than fifteen or sixteen came over to speak to us. Their English was impeccable and it wasn't long before they told us that they were mad about the Beatles. We showed them our song books and they joined us in a campfire sing-along Australian style. One young and very attractive blonde girl told us that she thought that Rob had a Cockney accent which we thought very perceptive on her part. She also told us that she was living with her parents in a summer house about fifteen kilometres away but she appeared to have been camping with a couple of boys not much older than herself. This seemed to have been quite unusual to us at the time.

Next day we motored all day arriving at Falkenborg where we purchased more provisions before continuing on to Halsingborg, driving straight to the quay to book a ferry to Copenhagen. We were amused when we noticed that the only other car with GB plates on the ferry was occupied by three Chinese gentlemen.

Arriving at Halsingborg we found that the camping ground was crowded and the only available site was adjacent to the men's toilet block. It was impossible to get a good night's sleep as our peace was punctuated throughout the night by the loud banging of doors, the continual flushing of toilets and the guttural oaths of men with full bladders tripping over our guy ropes in their haste to relieve themselves in the toilets. Just for good measure it rained all night without any sign of respite

DENMARK

Having driven off the Halsingborg Ferry we covered the fifty kilometres to Copenhagen, eventually making our camp on the City's outskirts. As we were operating on tight budgets we noticed how cheap grocery items were in Denmark by comparison to Sweden. The people were extremely friendly and helpful and went out of their way to be of assistance when it was needed.

Again it rained all night providing no incentive for us to get up early in the morning. However the weather improved as the day progressed encouraging us to make a late start into the city's capital.

After an initial look around and a meal costing six shillings per person we allowed ourselves to indulge in large glasses of Danish lager, our first alcoholic beverage since leaving England over two weeks before.

Our stay in Copenhagen lasted three days which enabled us to enjoy the Harbour and Hans Christian Andersen's 'Little Mermaid'. For me it brought back nostalgic memories of my previous visit to that city as a British National serviceman following the completion of a NATO military exercise in October, 1957. Naturally we also visited the Tivoli Gardens and endeavoured to soak up the light hearted atmosphere enjoyed by millions of people over the years.

Our last day in Copenhagen was spent checking the vehicles, washing our clothing and taking advantage of the low price of foods with which to stock up.

On my previous visit to Denmark I could never have imagined that seven years hence I would be making the journey from Denmark to Germany in another army vehicle over exactly the same route as in 1957. It then really struck me that life could be filled with mysteries which added an aspect to life that I had begun not only to recognise but to also greatly appreciate as well.

Driving from Odense we made straight for the German border, crossing at Flensborg.

Part Four
EUROPE
Germany - Switzerland
Italy - Greece - Turkey

GERMANY

Having travelled about a hundred and fifty kilometres since crossing the German border we pulled up at a campsite but found that the camping fees were too high. It was therefore agreed that we should press on towards Hamburg. By late evening we still had been unable to find a suitable site for the night but as we were in need of a rest we sought sanctuary in a lay-by just off the main autobahn. After a short break we decided that as the prospect of finding a campsite had diminished we would spend the night there.

At 10.00pm we had a visit from the local Police Highway Patrol who appeared not to have been worried about our presence, presumably thinking that by our appearance we must have been students engaged in a lengthy holiday travelling through Europe. They left us as we prepared to sleep in the vehicles. The occupants of the roomier Bedford fared far better than the Jeep dwellers where conditions were extremely cramped. We had to contend not only with the steering wheel but with three gear levers and a hand brake, not to mention luggage stowed in every conceivable spare crevice. After a while I realised that sleep would be hard to come by under these conditions so I decided to roll out my sleeping bag on the grass verge and grab as much sleep as possible although this was interrupted spasmodically by the noise of heavy trucks and a few cars whose drivers required the use of nearby toilets.

Needless to say we made an early start next day and headed straight for Hamburg. I had previously been to Hamburg but driving through that city on this occasion the only landmark I was able to recognise was the towering statue of Bismarck.

Driving south we soon reached the outskirts of Luneburg which for me engendered many feelings of nostalgia as it was there that I had spent most of my days as a national serviceman in the British Army. The weather was warm and sunny and the scenery on Luneburg Heath where incidentally Field Marshall Montgomery had received the German surrender in May, 1945, was as beautiful as I had previously remembered it. After a long day's drive we pulled off the autobahn and travelled through Gottingen, finally finding a place in the open, surrounded by undulating hills on which small clumps of trees nestled amongst fields of crops as far as the eye could see; a perfect place in which to rest for the night.

As the evening shadows lengthened we walked to the local guesthouse for a drink. The beer looked weak but belied its potency. We slept well.

The drive south to Frankfurt was uneventful except for a puncture in the LVW Jeep. The Jeep was equipped with split rim wheels which were supposed to facilitate speedy repairs, particularly punctures. The four centre bolts could be removed to enable the rims to be split in two thus allowing the tyre and inner tubes to be removed and repaired without the use of tyre levers. However the rims were never able to live up to their designers' expectations. Having removed the central bolts the rims were extremely difficult to split and involved a great deal of force. Having repaired a puncture and reassembled the rims, the inner tubes often used to become pinched causing yet another puncture.

I recall that during my time in the army the vehicle mechanics used to inflate the split rim tyre with a powerful pump to such a pressure that the rims would split apart. On one occasion the two rims refused to budge so more air was pumped into the inner tube. Suddenly there was an almighty BANG forcing the split rims to part with such force that one of them ploughed through a nearby brick wall, much to the consternation of the major who was in charge of the service centre.

We spent some time in Frankfurt where Geoff decided to take a group photograph using the old castle wall as a background. With meticulous care he placed us all exactly where he wanted us to be and set the camera on a delayed action exposure. Having pressed the button on the camera he darted back to where we were standing but at that very moment we all vacated our positions leaving Geoff to be the only person left. The result was a startled Geoff being the only person in the photo.

Although we commenced the next part of our journey in convoy, Rob, our navigator managed to get lost leaving the remaining two vehicles to drive on to our next destination. Fortunately the Bedford eventually found its way out of Frankfurt, joining the rest of the party at a camp site in Heidelberg where, upon enquiry we learned that the local camping ground had no vacancies.

Shortly afterwards we found ourselves looking down at the beautiful floodlit castle of Heidelberg and felt that we shouldn't miss this opportunity to admire the castle at closer range. The extensive ruins of the castle overlooked the old town and we found it hard to imagine what it would have been like clothed in its original splendour six hundred years before.

Having developed (or nurtured) a certain taste for German beer we came across a local guest house where a couple of our number succumbed to the effects of the local brew to the point where they were so inebriated that they joined some American servicemen in a sing along. We finally left the American GI's quite late and found ourselves facing the prospect of finding a place to sleep as almost impossible. However we did succeed in locating another lay-by where we put Jack and Brian to bed on the ground before the remainder of our party spent the night trying to get some sleep in our respective vehicles.

Next morning, the 21st July, we awoke to warm weather and radiant sunshine. We gladly quit the cramped conditions in the Jeeps for the gentle morning air. As we had planned to arrive in Switzerland in a day or two we knew that we would soon be negotiating mountainous terrain and that our rather well worn vehicles would have to prove equal to the task before us. We therefore checked them over before commencing the day's journey. The weather had become very hot by the time we reached Baden-Baden which prompted us to dive into the cool, health giving waters for a well earned swim.

Nestling in the foothills of the Black Forest Baden-Baden had once been renowned as the summer capital of Europe. In the nineteenth century it had boasted many well known frequent visitors including Wilhelm 1st of Germany, Berlioz, Brahms and even Queen Victoria. At the time I tried to picture the rather regal figure of The Queen escorted by her retinue and wondered whether they had brought with them Her Majesty's bathing machine in which she used to maintain her modesty whilst taking to the waters near Osborne House on the Isle of Wight. I tried to imagine her entourage endeavouring to drag her cumbersome bathing machine into the clear, still waters of Baden-Baden.

Driving up the steep hills within the Black Forest proved somewhat of a challenge for our vehicles. The Bedford's radiator boiled, emitting steam into the cab but upon inspection we found that the radiator cap had not been firmly secured. Also the LVW Jeep started to whine but after a thorough check we traced the noise to the gearbox which was low on oil. Having topped up the gearbox with oil it quietened down. We then proceeded on towards the Swiss border.

SWITZERLAND

On the 22nd of July we completed our climb through the Black Forest crossing the border into Switzerland at Schaffhausen. In spite of our initial problems the vehicles had performed well although we felt relieved to have arrived at our evening camp site on the banks of the River Rhine. However our relief was short lived as no sooner had we erected our tents and brewed some tea than we were invaded by swarms of flies and wasps. Preparing and eating an evening meal became a contest between us, the flies and the wasps. Needless to say we were more than happy to leave the site next morning as we pressed on towards Zurich, arriving late morning in order to pick up our mail from the local American Express Office. Although we did spend some time in Zurich we were becoming less inclined to explore cities, finding the rural areas far more to our liking.

Having completed our business in Zurich we made our way out of the city eventually camping in a picturesque valley at Oberarth in the region dominated by the beautiful Lake Lucerne. After the rush and bustle of the city it was a restful experience to enjoy the breathtaking serenity of the countryside where the only noise to be heard was the sound of cowbells.

We were on the road again early the next day knowing that the day's drive would be a strenuous one for the vehicles, particularly for the old Jeeps, and so it proved to be. As the gradients up the St Gotthard Pass were very severe in places the LVW Jeep in which Jack and I were travelling was struggling and holding up traffic behind us. These Jeeps were equipped with a low range booster gear for difficult or mountainous terrain but their design was such that to engage the low booster gear the driver was required to engage four wheel drive mode as well. Thus, instead of changing gear with just one gearstick we had the challenge of having three. Moving our feet and manipulating the gear sticks required some dexterity on our part and Jack and I joked that playing the organ in Westminster Abbey might have been just a bit easier than this.

Another problem lay in the fact that under these circumstances the front and rear wheels were not always exactly synchronised, causing 'overwind'. As a consequence every couple of hundred metres the vehicle would 'hop' as the front and rear wheels became out of sync.

Having successfully negotiated the St Gotthard Pass we arrived at Pont Teresa on the Italian border late in the evening. The camp site at Lake Lugarno being quite expensive Geoff, Anne and Brian decided just before dusk to look for a free site in the area leaving Jerry, Lyn, Rob, Jack and myself at the initial site. It was very peaceful camping on the banks of this picturesque lake especially as we could swim out for about a hundred metres to experience the clear warm water lapping over our bodies. Looking towards the shore we were able to admire the surrounding scenery. It was breathtaking.

In the late afternoon the five of us who had remained at the original campsite drove to a wooded area just the other side of Pont Teresa where we were later joined by Geoff, Anne and Brian.

ITALY

We crossed the border into Italy before midday and continued driving south in blazing sunshine where the temperatures stayed around the high thirties (Celsius) mark which made a welcome change from the weather we had experienced in Scandinavia.

By early evening we had driven down to Genoa during which time we had been able to observe the style of the Italians' driving. They all appeared to have been under the illusion that they were competing in a Grand Prix race and not merely travelling from point A to point B. However the hectic day's drive revealed its reward when we eventually found a quiet camp site well off the beaten track at Carasco. The area was very peaceful and being quite close to the sea we were able to enjoy the bright sunshine tempered by a gentle sea breeze. We decided to stay here for a while, particularly after having sampled a two litre bottle of local wine which cost only four shillings.

As the town of Chiavari was only about seven kilometres from where we were camping, Brian and I decided to take an early morning walk in that direction. Eventually the town came into view as we looked down onto the mouth of the Entello River with its fertile planes on either side and Castello di Chiavari in the background.

Walking through the outskirts of the town we noticed attractive little piazzas as well as some imposing homes and some more modest but nevertheless very attractive dwellings. Finding a small green grocers shop we purchased a huge succulent melon which we took back to our camp for everyone to share.

As the Jeeps were looking somewhat the worse for wear after their recent exertions Jack, Geoff and I spent the afternoon checking them over and carrying out minor repairs. In the evening Jerry, Rob Lyn and Anne walked into the nearby town leaving Jack, Brian, Geoff and myself in camp sharing a bottle of the local wine.

The next morning heralded a change in the weather and by noon the heavens had opened unleashing a huge thunder storm bringing with it torrents of rain, in fact we measured seven centimetres within the first hour which necessitated our digging deep trenches around the tents to enable the water to run off and to protect our sleeping quarters.

Although we were inconvenienced by the rain we had already started to appreciate this part of the world and felt that we needed to slow our progress a little in order to absorb the beauty and enjoyment that coastal Italy had to offer.

Just seventy kilometres along the coastal road we arrived at Marina Di Massa where we decided to camp within a pine wood and adjacent to a picturesque beach. Needless to say with the Mediterranean just a few metres from our camp we had little hesitation in deciding to stay on the Tuscan Riviera for a while, soaking up the atmosphere and swimming whenever the mood arose. We could have asked for nothing more. As the sun sank over the horizon each evening we became fascinated as thousands of fireflies lit up the fir trees, the like of which we had not seen since our last Christmas in England.

However, all was not well for an undernourished little kitten that came into our camp shortly after our arrival. Lyn, ever the practical member of the party, rummaged through the stores in the Bedford and found a tin of sardines. Having opened the can she drained off the oil and carefully washed the contents before giving it to the kitten which ate voraciously until there was none left. As we held it in our arms and stroked its soft fur it was very rewarding to hear the poor little animal purr very softly, probably the only time it had ever purred during its short life. It was with feelings of sadness that we left Marina Di Massa. We left it some food but wondered what would become of the kitten and hoped that some kind person would take it under their wing and give it a good home. However we needed to press on to our next location which was Pisa.

We were certainly not disappointed with the sights of Pisa for it was difficult to believe that its tower could lean at such an angle without actually toppling over particularly as in 1964 the remedial work on the tower was yet to be carried out. However we were allowed to walk up the steps as far as the fourth level. There were hardly any people around and there was no charge to enter. Nearly fifty years later I revisited Pisa which on that occasion was thronged with visitors who were allowed for a fee to mount the steps to the bell tower, the much needed remedial work having been carried out to the foundations a few years before.

Having camped at Follonica that night we pressed on towards Rome. During that day LVW Jeep had developed a noticeable wheel wobble which we eventually eliminated by diagonally changing the tyres around. Naturally we wanted to spend as much time as we could in Rome but obviously didn't want to park our vehicles there due to security concerns. We therefore camped at a site about twenty kilometres from the city that was tailor-made for our purposes being next to the sea, not overcrowded and very close to a railway station where trains could convey us to Rome.

Rob and Jack volunteered to stay in camp that day leaving Jerry, Lyn, Anne, Geoff, Brian and myself to catch the train into the Capital. Rome certainly fulfilled our expectations as we marvelled at the skill and ingenuity of a nation that had been at its zenith of power two thousand years before.

At the time I had been reading 'A Short History of The World' by H G Wells and had become acquainted with Pope Innocent the 11th. When visiting the Vatican the very next day I came across the embalmed body of that very same Pope. It felt how very strange to actually see him hundreds of years later. He didn't look at all well.

On the way to Naples next morning we stopped at Cassino, the site of one of the bloodiest battles of the Second World War. The German and Allied Armies had been locked in the battle of Monte Cassino for several months as the opposing sides strove to capture the monastery which, being at the top of a hill dominated the country below. I tried to picture the scene when the battle had raged twenty years before and thought of my closest friend in England whose father was killed nearby in 1944. My friend's only memory of his father had been when waving goodbye to him at Waterloo Railway Station as Gunner Cyril Humphrey boarded a train to return to his army unit.

Naples was a great disappointment. We witnessed poverty stricken barefoot young beggars running around outside shanty shacks, jumping onto the buffers of local trams. To us they seemed to have occupied a social universe far removed from the opulence of Rome and The Vatican. These religious institutions whilst preaching love and compassion appeared to care little for the practical needs of the most vulnerable and needy members of their flock.

By early afternoon we had arrived in Pompeii. On our arrival Jack had decided that he had seen enough 'heaps of rubble that looked like bomb sites' and so decided to stay with the vehicles. It was unfortunate that he had reached a saturation point at the time but we were thankful to him for staying with the vehicles during our absence.

As with most visitors we found the ruins quite fascinating and were amazed at how well preserved they were. We found it barely believable that the city, buried beneath four metres of ash and pumice during an eruption in the first century A D could have remained undiscovered until almost seventeen-hundred years later. The Forum, streets and gardens were well preserved as were the plaster casts of the victims in their last moments of life after the eruption of Vesuvius. It was a reminder of the sheer power of that volcanic eruption almost two thousand years before. The fact that the cataclysm failed to destroy the frescos was also amazing and how wonderful it was to have witnessed first-hand a well preserved glimpse of life in Roman times.

Having returned to the vehicles and assembled our convoy we proceeded to Sorrento where we camped the night.

Next day, the 9th August we left Sorrento in the morning, driving over the mountain road to Salerno before turning inland towards Potenza. Not wishing to pitch our tents too near to civilization we decided to camp rough on the other side of the town. The picturesque scenery was marked by steep hills which gradually melded into an undulating landscape. By now we were certainly enjoying the prospect of day after day of unbroken sunshine and clear blue skies, the rain and generally soggy conditions of Scandinavia having evaporated from our memories by the heat of the Italian summer.

We were now keen to move on towards Greece which necessitated booking the vehicles onto the ferry at Brindisi. At Brindisi we camped near to the sea port having arrived at 7.00 pm.

The following morning Geoff and Rob drove into the town in order to book the ferry to Greece whilst the rest of the party busied themselves with laundering clothing and servicing the other two vehicles. We felt some relief when Geoff and Rob returned with the news that they had secured bookings for all three vehicles for departure at 10 o'clock that night.

At 7.30pm we drove out from the camp site but barely a kilometre from the ferry terminal Jeep LVW suddenly gasped and stopped. We opened the bonnet, crawled underneath and carried out a few diagnostic tests which revealed that a joint in the fuel pipe had fractured. As we were left with limited time and still needed to refuel the vehicles, Geoff towed the stricken Jeep to a service station where each vehicle was filled up with fuel. Fortunately we were able to effect a temporary repair to the fuel line and were able to drive the vehicles onto the ferry on time.

The ferry trip from Brindisi to Igoumenitsa in Greece was uneventful although Jack and I were worried that the temporary repair to the Jeep might not hold. Fortunately our apprehensions turned out to have been unjustified.

GREECE

On arrival on the 12th August we were elated when we switched on the ignition on LVW Jeep, activated the electric auxiliary fuel pump and managed to start the engine. The temporary repair to the fuel line was holding.

Having changed money into the local drachma in Igoumenitsa and purchased more fuel, we drove out into the neighbouring countryside. It was beautiful, unspoiled land with rocky hills, sprinklings of trees and bushes with steeper hills in the background. By late afternoon we had reached Ioannina, a quaint little village with many narrow streets with old houses on either side. At a little village store we purchased over five pounds of grapes and two pounds of peaches for the paltry sum of two shillings.

We heard from the locals that there were some interesting caves nearby and some of our number decided to visit them. However as Brian and I were in some need of a haircut we visited the local barber and having been shorn the shop floor resembled an Australian sheep shearing shed at the end of a day's shearing. People were very friendly and took Brian and myself for Germans on account of our blond hair and blue eyes. In the meantime a local farmer invited the other members of the group to camp on his land, an offer they readily accepted.

We were up and dressed early next morning to the very rural sound of sheep bells. By this time we had decided to make permanent repairs to the LVW Jeep's fuel line. However our work was somewhat hampered by the 'helping hands' of some of the local men and boys who were intrigued when we lit the petrol stove, placed the soldering iron on the flames, only to then disappear under the vehicle, solder in one hand and hot soldering iron in the other. After the repair had been carried out and the engine started, no further fuel leaks were found. As we emerged from under the Jeep we were fascinated by the spectre of a woman spinning wool astride a donkey as she passed by.

Having once again packed up our belongings we climbed aboard the vehicles and drove on towards Arta, passing by a superb lake with dozens of hills on either side forming an enormous bay of brilliant blue water. The bay resembled a giant pot of ink, so vivid was its colour.

We eventually came upon the village of Aitolikon and wishing to capture the local atmosphere we paid a visit to the local church whilst Geoff, Anne, Lyn and Rob went in search of the local post office in order to buy some stamps. The local Post Master must have been a person of some influence and prestige as he ordered his employees to give up their chairs whilst inviting the travellers to enjoy a glass of freshly squeezed lemon juice with him. He chatted with them about their journey and having been told that there were other members in the party he sent someone to find us. Thus, we all chatted most amicably (mainly in rather rusty French) for some time in his office, sipping cool lemon juice. When he found out that we wanted to do some shopping he sent for a young man who was fluent in English.

Anthony duly arrived and wasted no time in taking us around the local shops. He was a tall, well built young man of about twenty years of age with dark hair, clear skin, very good looks and a great personality to match. Having completed our shopping accompanied by at least a score of children, we purchased a large bottle of beer which we requested be delivered to the Post Master with our thanks for his kindness and concern for our wellbeing.

By then we were assembled in the street admiring the view of the nearby lake when the Post Master appeared bringing with him the local Magistrate. Following a short conversation between Anthony, the Post Master and the Magistrate, we were told that we would be directed to a suitable spot where we would be able to set up our camp and that they had also arranged a moonlight boat trip on the lagoon for us that evening. The campsite turned out to be the local children's playground at the end of the village.

Erecting our tents was an experience never to be forgotten. Children of every shape and size scurried to and fro hampering our endeavours under the earnest misapprehension that they were being useful. We drove the tent pegs in at least a dozen times only to be dislodged by small boys tripping over the guy ropes. At last some semblance of order was restored as our shattered nerves felt the need for some alcoholic sustenance.

However, further mayhem was in store as we marshalled our pots, pans and stoves in preparation for our evening meal. Old ladies appeared from nowhere giving us the benefit of their advice on how to boil potatoes and vegetables. One would advise that the flame was too high only to be countermanded by another that it was in fact too low. The whole scene reminded me of the picnic scene in Jerome K Jerome's novel 'Three Men in a Boat' written over a hundred years before.

After a hurried meal (including a saucepan of under-done potatoes) the boat arrived to transport us across the lake. Anthony then proclaimed the boat to be too small which wasn't surprising since the whole village had aspired to undertake the voyage. However, the numbers were eventually whittled down and the trip commenced. Nevertheless the vessel was still very overcrowded and our bottoms perched precariously over the gunwales as we took a thorough soaking.

The evening was surely one of the most memorable and spectacular that any of us had ever experienced. The night was perfect with not a cloud in a sky that was sporadically illuminated by vivid trails of shooting stars every few seconds, lighting up the heavens like an ethereal fireworks display.

As there was a high concentration of phosphor in the water, the vessel left a phosphorescent glow in its wake and the oars resembled gigantic white hot pokers as they dipped into the calm waters of the lagoon. This magical scene was made even more memorable as the young men sang traditional Greek songs in perfect harmony. We were told that one song contained a hundred and seventy verses. Luckily we heard only the abridged version.

We retired to bed at midnight after thanking our most hospitable Greek friends for such kindness. It truly had been a day to remember.

14th August - My 27th Birthday.

We left Aitolikon at 9.15 am and by midday had arrived at Antirno where we ferried the vehicles for a short crossing, arriving at Rio a short time later. After another short drive we ended up at the small village of Aigo.

Having scouted around for a suitable camping venue we called in at the local general store to make enquiries. The owner was extremely friendly and as luck would have it invited us to camp on his land on condition that any supplies we required during our stay would be purchased at his shop. We readily agreed particularly as he appeared to stock a wide range of merchandise including the locally made Ouzo.

The land on which were camped was just a short way up an escarpment overlooking a pebbly beach that led down to a most spectacular view of crystal clear sea. Looking across the still water we could see the opposite shore where distant hills stood out against a backdrop of white cumulus clouds.

By now the weather was becoming more settled the further south we travelled and armed with this confidence we decided to leave the tents in the vehicles. Instead we each drove upright posts into the ground, attached our mosquito nets and having inflated our 'Lilo' mattresses, threw our sleeping bags onto the beds ready to sleep under the stars for the first time on the trip. The prospect of sleeping in the open in such an exotic environment was quite exciting.

We hastily completed a few remaining chores before donning our swimming gear and making for the beach a few metres away. Having swum out about only twenty metres or so we glanced back towards the shore and with the aid of our snorkels were amazed to see such an array of local marine life beneath us. However, what was even more spectacular was to observe how steeply the beach fell away from the shoreline. It felt as though we were swimming along the side of a huge mountain which fell away into infinity.

In the evening Jack prepared a birthday meal but the highlight of the day was to sleep under the stars for the first time on the journey. It was a memorable birthday for me, my slumbers doubtless being assisted by the odd glass of Ouzo prior to climbing under the mozzie net.

We were so captivated by the unspoiled beauty of Aigio that we decided to stay for a few days although we did venture into nearby Patrai one afternoon but were disappointed that most of the shops and cafes there were closed. Nevertheless we were keen to avail ourselves of the many recreational opportunities in Aigio especially swimming in the cool clear water which was so close to our camp site. One afternoon Rob and I swam across the bay to a little village and emerging from the water we came across several modest but picturesque whitewashed houses dotted about the hinterland. Walking through the narrow streets we both remarked how time seemed to have passed by this little village. There was a conspicuous absence of motor vehicles and as a consequence the streets were quiet apart from the occasional sound of a donkey braying.

For an hour or so we soaked up the ambient peace and tranquillity before taking to the water again to swim the four or five hundred metres back to camp.

Having spent three wonderful days at Aigio we packed the vehicles, bade farewell to the shopkeeper and made our way towards Corinth. Perhaps our expectations of this famous biblical area had been too high for we found the town which Saint Paul had visited almost two thousand years before to be very disappointing. Having previously witnessed the commercialisation of such iconic places as the Vatican we should have been inured from disappointment. However, Corinth struck us as being so commercial that we were only too happy to move on to Athens after a very short stay.

We drove to within fifteen kilometres of Athens and were most impressed by our view of the famous city. Athens, nestling in a basin, its bleached buildings dominated by the Parthenon taking centre stage was certainly a sight to behold. In the distance we could see the home of Socrates which evoked a short history lesson from Jack who informed us that the said man of wisdom had ended his days dying from an overdose of 'wedlock'.

As the evening shadows lengthened we concluded that we had run out of time in which to find a suitable camping site and had to resort to 'roughing it' overnight, eventually camping next to a rubbish dump situated on a hill overlooking the city and adjacent to a busy road, an airport and some latrines.

We managed to ensconce ourselves in a somewhat more salubrious camp site for the next couple of days and spent most of our stay visiting the famous landmarks of this historic city. After three wonderfully interesting days it was time to take the Thessalonica Road. The journey for the next three hundred kilometres that day included a mixture of rough unmade roads and hilly mountain tracks until we finally came upon a free camping site not far from Farsala on the 21st August.

The following morning Jack, Rob and I got up at dawn and serviced the LVW Jeep and Bedford prior to starting the day's drive a few hours later, stopping for a lunch break in the early afternoon. We had no sooner stepped from the vehicles when a local inhabitant stopped his donkey cart and engaged us in conversation. He was very friendly, probably in his forties and was later joined by his two friends who were also farm labourers. When it was time for them to leave they insisted that we accept a couple of bags of freshly harvested onions and some rich, juicy tomatoes.

Shopping at Thessalonica was a revelation as provisions at the markets were very inexpensive, especially fruit and vegetables, with freshly picked peaches being purchased for three pence per pound. As we were making our purchases a little boy sidled up to us and whispered "Beatles".

Upon leaving Thessalonica we drove about twenty-five kilometres where we camped by the still waters of a lake. The area we had selected was very much to our liking but also to the liking of a large number of small mosquitoes that were intent upon varying their diet with a dash of young British blood. We were more than ready to seek the sanctuary of our sleeping bags that night having tucked the bottom of our mosquito nets firmly under our inflatable 'Lilo' beds. We slept well accompanied by the sound of frustrated mosquitoes buzzing into the netting under which we had taken refuge.

We were awoken somewhat earlier than planned the next day by some small boys asking for cigarettes. As none of us smoked they disappeared only to re-appear a short time later with their families, one member of which produced a mandolin that he played whilst two rather poorly dressed women performed a rather strange belly dance. However, at that time of the day we were in no mood for entertainment and also suspicious that the locals possessed ulterior motives.

It took us little time for us to pack up our belongings and move on, driving about fifty kilometres to a very large beach with sand dunes that were dotted with small bushes extending down to the sea. The sea was of a greenish colour in stark contrast to the deep blue we had previously encountered but our camp site offered excellent prospects for swimming as the beach sloped away very gradually until meeting the tide.

As the area was totally secluded I decided to crouch behind one of the large bushes in order to answer an urgent call of nature. As I was attending to the job in hand I heard the engine of a motor vehicle some way off but as the noise came closer I began to worry. I became even more worried when the sound of the engine appeared to be heading in my direction impelling me to rush out with my buttocks exposed and my shorts around my ankles, still clutching a toilet roll. My retreat was not a moment too soon as I beheld a Fiat 600 car with GB plates actually demolishing the bush behind which I had been hiding. The driver, a young Englishman, was almost as startled as I had been at this turn of events. He apologised profusely as he explained that he had been driving over the bushes 'for a bit of fun!'

In the evening we visited a local village for a soft drink and a look around before going back to camp, enjoying a moonlight swim and then tucking ourselves under our mosquito nets for the night.

It had always been our intention to swap vehicles crews around in order to maintain harmony within the group, an arrangement which was working well and added credence to the maxim that a change is as good as a holiday.

The next morning it was my turn to drive the LVW Jeep with Brian as my passenger. Brian was very easy to get along with and being of a similar age we had quite a lot in common. Brian had just completed his studies in dentistry and was looking forward to employment at a dental practice in the Newport-Pagnell area just south of Northampton. He had recently become engaged to a local young lady but wanted to travel the world before eventually settling down to family life and full-time employment. He was fortunate enough to have met Geoff Kirk at the time that the overland trip was in its embryonic stage.

On this particular day, the 24th August, we arrived at Elefthesoupolis where we changed more money into Greek drachma. Our journey then took us along narrow country roads where we observed tobacco leaves curing in the sun outside almost every house in each village through which we passed. We eventually arrived at Alexandroupolis where we purchased some provisions. After another hour's drive we decided to camp in some shrub land before crossing over the border into Turkey the following day.

Part Five

ASIA

Turkey - Iran - West Pakistan India
Himalayas - Nepal
East Pakistan - Burma
Thailand - Malaysia - Singapore

TURKEY

We had now been on the road for eight weeks and had driven through three Scandinavian and five European countries and were now very much aware that we were on the cusp of some new and exciting experiences as we approached Turkey and the gateway to Asia.

Having quit our overnight camp we drove towards the Turkish border, eventually crossing at Ipsala. Almost immediately we noticed a difference not only in the terrain but also in the way of life. The countryside appeared more arid. We saw camels and tortoises for the first time. Also we could not help but observe that the first local inhabitants we saw were a man walking along the street with a woman walking a few paces behind. Given that fifty years before, Kemal Ataturk had guided Turkey from an almost feudal country ruled by the sultans into a democratic westernised society, the spectacle was most surprising.

The dusty road on which we first drove was unsealed but to make matters worse, tar had been poured onto the road, presumably as a prelude to its being resurfaced. However as the sun was still beating down upon it, the road had become a glutinous black mess. Our vehicles churned up the tar which annealed itself to the underside of the Jeeps and Bedford, not to mention cloying our clothing, legs, hands and arms as well.

After negotiating the wet tar we then graduated onto a dusty unmade sandy road where the vehicles again churned up the dust which then glued itself onto the Jeeps and Bedford as well as our clothing. The dust became so intense that we were hard put to see the vehicle in front of us.

As we needed Turkish currency we stopped at a small town where we came across a bank. Looking decidedly scruffy and unkempt except for Anne who had somehow managed to evade the tar and dust, we were all ushered into the bank manager's office where the business was transacted in French. With tar and sand stuck to our legs and clothing not to mention matted into our hair, we would have put even the most disreputable urchins in a Dickens novel to shame. To make matters worse, the manager was a picture of sartorial elegance dressed in a beautifully tailored brown suit that would have flattered even the likes of Beau Brummel as he sat in his air conditioned office.

We were happy to leave the bank with Turkish lire in our pockets and continued our drive towards Istanbul. En route we found that the local people were very friendly. Many workers looked up from their work of harvesting sunflower seeds in order to wave to us. At a small village we purchased melons and tomatoes at what appeared to us to have been ridiculously low prices.

Eventually having driven the coastal road we camped near a beach at Silivri about forty kilometres west of Istanbul. We were now becoming accustomed to clear blue skies. Looking out over the Sea of Marmara the sky was similar to the crystal clarity we had experienced when entering Greece. However the cloudless sky was to herald a very cold night.

After driving over rough roads and still looking very scruffy, not to mention the vehicles which still had tar and sand plastered all over them, we decided to service the vehicles and wash some clothing before driving into Istanbul. After arriving in Istanbul we established ourselves at the BP Motorcamp ten kilometres from the city centre.

Feeling a little more presentable in our clean clothes and swept out vehicles we then drove into Istanbul city centre noting how adventurous were the local motorists where road rules appeared to have been observed on an 'ad hoc' basis depending upon the mood of the driver. Having parked the vehicles, we stepped out onto the pavement and into another world. Whilst still on the fringes of Europe it felt as though we were not only already in Asia but back into mediaeval times as well where many of the buildings had been constructed when the old Ottoman Empire was at its peak.

Prior to setting out on the journey from England we had arranged for mail to be sent to us at the various American Express Offices en route. We called at the American Express Office in Istanbul and duly collected our mail and were intrigued to find that Jack had received a parcel from England. With great anticipation Jack opened the parcel that had been sent by a friend and to our amazement he found that it contained a can of bacon. None of us had tasted bacon since the previous June although some of us might have had visions of such a delicacy in our dreams. I am sure Jack would love to have crept away into a corner to consume the whole can himself but as we stood around salivating at the prospect of titillating our palates with such a luxury, Jack emptied the contents of the can into a frying pan and gave us equal portions of this veritable treasure trove.

As evening approached we hastened to locate the famous Blue Mosque and managed to find a suitable vantage point from which to witness the spectacle of its legendary sunset. With the Mosque in the foreground we watched in awe as the sun slowly receded over the horizon bathing the dome and its minarets against the background of a deep crimson glow until eventually the whole building itself became a silhouette with the darkness of night in the background.

Not far from the Blue Mosque we came across a back street that time seemed to have passed by. The timber buildings with miniature patios on either side of narrow cobbled streets presented a microcosm of life in that the city in years gone by. It could almost have been a scene from the Arabian Nights with Ali Baba, Sinbad and Aladdin likely to have materialised at any moment. Strangely, even though the scene was so foreign to us we nevertheless felt very safe as the local people were so very friendly.

We made our way down to the harbour and had our first view of Asia on the other side of the Bosporus but as evening was drawing near we headed for the Golden Horn Bridge and back to our camp site.

Whilst we had admired the Blue Mosque at nightfall, we had yet to view it from the inside. Next morning, having removed our shoes outside the building, we slipped silently inside. We were not disappointed. The interior was completely bereft of seating and the superb decorations under its vast dome looked down upon a magnificent carpeted floor.

Outside the Mosque we found Geoff who advised us that the RYF Jeep had blown a cylinder head gasket that would require replacement before the next leg of the journey.

Next day we inspected all three vehicles and discovered that the LVW Jeep's heavy duty battery had sprung a leak in one of its cells. Jack and I tried to repair it but as all the other cells were sound we deemed the problem to have been of only a minor nature.

ASIA

On the 28th of August after a last trip into the city we boarded a ferry over the Bosporus, saying 'farewell' to Europe. Following a short ferry ride we stepped onto Asian soil for the very first time. At that time I could never have imagined that it would be over eight years before I would see Europe again.

We took the road to Ankara and drove a further eighty kilometres before camping 'rough' by the roadside.

By morning the weather had changed and instead of the warm sunshine of Istanbul, a chill rain had taken its place to make the day's journey very uncomfortable. However, in spite of the wet and cold conditions we made good time through the mountainous terrain that eventually gave way to gentler hills overlooking coniferous forests below.

No sooner had we stopped for a lunch break on the brow of a hill than three very poorly clad lads came near. They were a pathetic sight. Their trousers had stood a great deal of patching and were frayed beyond description, hanging off them like rags. Their dusty old clothes appeared inadequate for anything but the mildest of weather as they huddled together against the rain and cold. We shared a hot meal with them and they in turn gave us some branches on which were some berries. We wondered how these poor souls would cope with the severity of a Turkish winter.

Ironically, a few kilometres further on, we came across a ballistic missile site obviously costing millions of pounds and erected for the destruction of humanity. The contrast between man's amazing ability to manipulate his environment and his pitiful incompetence at properly managing his own affairs was never more starkly defined than by these two phenomena. Our world of nylon and atomic energy was still for some, a world of poverty.

Fortunately for us the next hundred and sixty kilometres drive heralded the start of much warmer weather so that when we set up camp not far from Ankara the temperature had risen quite markedly.

The 30th of August was a day that started rather badly, particularly for Jack and me when the LVW Jeep stubbornly refused to start. We finally resorted to push starting the heavy Jeep which proved difficult as we were parked on sandy soil and the weather was very hot. Eventually the engine reluctantly spluttered into life but it soon became apparent that an engine valve had burnt out.

Working on a side valve engine as opposed to overhead valve models presents certain problems. With an overhead valve engine, the cylinder head can be removed and repairs carried out on a work bench. However to repair a side valve engine the work has to be done in a confined space under the bonnet of the vehicle, in fact to be a contortionist would have been a quite an asset.

We removed the cylinder head without much trouble. Having removed the burnt out valve and ground in a replacement valve with the aid of valve grinding paste, we compressed the valve spring with a special valve lifting tool and inserted the two tiny collets into grooves around the stem of the valve, securing them temporarily in place with thick engine grease. Under normal circumstances the collets would have stayed in place until the compressing tool had been released but to our horror tragedy struck!

As I gently released the valve lifter so that the little collets could nestle permanently into their allotted grooves, one of them became dislodged and pinged off somewhere into the desert sand. The loss of such a tiny engine part posed a huge threat to our journey as the chances of obtaining other collets would have been very slim. Unfortunately we did not possess a magnet with which to entice the collet to the surface but were forced to crawl very gingerly on our hands and knees lightly fingering the desert floor, being careful not to bury the tiny collet even further into the sand. Our search took us on an ever increasing radius as we became more and more disconsolate. Over an hour later and quite some way from the stricken vehicle we located the errant part. We all breathed a huge sigh of relief as we once again very carefully inserted the collets into the groove and very slowly released the valve spring tool. Thankfully a catastrophe had been averted.

Unfortunately another problem then occurred. As we were replacing the cylinder head onto the engine block an oil pipe fractured. Fortunately we were able to bypass the oil filter with the same piece of tubing and the Jeep lived once again. However, just as we thought that our problems had come to an end we found that Geoff's RYF Jeep had suffered a broken fuel pipe that necessitated a temporary soldering job before we could continue the rest of the day's journey.

We found that Ankara was quite different from Istanbul as it was very modern by comparison. Our time there was confined to shopping for some necessities and also becoming caught up in a crowd that was watching a march past of the Turkish Army.

From Ankara we made good time along asphalt roads for about eighty kilometres, enjoying the scenery along the way. The ground was barren with rolling hills on either side of the road and mountains beyond. On the roadside we came across the carcass of a dead mule being torn apart by hungry vultures. We stopped the vehicles and spent some time watching the sight of these huge birds as they screeched at each other whilst tearing the flesh from the mule

After a refuelling stop we drove over unmade roads twisting and bending their way around the hilly countryside. The soil was parched but even though there were clouds in the sky there seemed little prospect of them raining on the sun scorched earth below.

We finally arrived at Yosgat although Jack and I were later than the rest of the party, having stopped for an hour or so on the way to mend a puncture. Unfortunately the others knew nothing of our plight due to the amount of dust and sand stirred up by our convoy.

The local inhabitants of Yosgat were very friendly. A German speaking local made us most welcome as did another person who spoke English. These two gentlemen conducted us around the town, helping us with our purchases. One of them even introduced Geoff to a master craftsman who made a new fuel line for the Jeep and with the help of a local silversmith installed it on the Jeep for the meagre sum of twelve shillings.

That evening we camped a few kilometres outside Yosgat where we came across a friendly shepherd who was happy to chat with us at length. Sadly we were unable to comprehend a word he had uttered.

After repairing a puncture we crawled under our respective mozzie nets to sleep under the stars. The memory of those night skies has been indelibly imprinted on my mind. As I looked up I could see millions of stars standing out like diamonds as far as the eye could see and the Milky Way which previously I had observed as a faint blur during my life in England now appeared as a dominant feature in the night sky. Having accustomed my eyes to the position of the stars I was then able to pick out several man-made satellites as they plied their way around the earth. And there were the inevitable shooting stars which sped across the night sky but upon reaching earth's atmosphere expired in a final blaze of light before disappearing into obscurity.

The next day would herald the first of September and we wondered what experiences would unfold in the coming month.

Having left Yosgat at 8.15 am we drove on very rough unmade roads the surface of which was so powdery that we could not avoid continually skidding, an experience quite similar to driving on the icy roads in Britain. On either side of the road were mountains of differing colours with the lower plains dotted with salt pans. As we passed through small villages we observed oxen laboriously pulling threshers around in circles as the local inhabitants looked at us in surprised amusement.

After a day's drive we reached the town of Sivas. Here we posted letters home before moving on to Zara where we camped overnight. That night was bitterly cold compelling us to sleep with one sleeping bag inside another whilst still in the open air but covered by our mosquito nets.

Just before retiring for the night, Rob and Jerry remarked that the Bedford had not been pulling very well that day so it was decided that I should ride in the Bedford the next day to enable me to listen to the engine in order to diagnose the problem. On the day's journey we checked the fuel pump for leaks and the jets in the carburettor but found no problems. However upon checking the electrics we found that the gap on the distributor points was too small. The problem was then easily fixed by adjusting the gap using feeler gauges. We finally reached Erzincan at nightfall where we set up camp a short distance from the village.

In the evening Brian and I walked into the town and spent a most enjoyable time there. A travelling fair had just arrived and as we were looking for some entertainment some Turkish military officers asked if we would like to join them. Although they spoke no English we were able to communicate in German. They were most friendly and would not allow us to buy drinks or coffee. Looking around it was quite strange to witness men smoking hookahs and there were even a few horse drawn Hansom cabs wheeling around the town square.

There was quite a lot of maintenance work to be carried out on the vehicles the next day as we were well aware that from now on conditions on the roads and tracks would deteriorate. We stripped the cylinder head off the Bedford and decarbonised the cylinders having assumed that the low octane petrol we had been using would have left heavy carbon deposits on the pistons. However the cylinders had not accumulated all that much carbon.

As the LVW Jeep had been losing power, its cylinder head was removed exposing a poorly seated valve. We duly replaced the valve, being extra careful when reinstalling it as we didn't want another lost collet episode.

As a reward for our day's labour and also to test out the vehicles we made a trip into Erzincan to buy some fruit and cakes. Upon our return to camp a fierce sand storm suddenly blew up spraying fine sand everywhere including into the Jeeps and even our bedding. Although we tried to shake the sand and dust out of our clothing and bedding, a residual amount of sand was still lingering in our sleeping bags making our rest quite uncomfortable that night.

On the fourth of September I joined Jerry and Lyn in the Bedford, leaving Rob to drive with Jack in the LVW Jeep, our initial destination being Agri. The roads were hilly and dusty prompting us to drive very slowly through ancient looking villages trying not to stir up too much dust and upsetting the locals. Driving in convoy had been almost impossible due to the dust clouds and it was inevitable that vehicles would become separated from time to time.

About forty kilometres from Agri, Jerry, Lyn and I realised that we had lost contact with the others and as it was becoming quite late we decided to set up our own camp in a secluded field and accordingly unloaded our kitchen utensils in preparation for a meal. No sooner had we placed the billy on the petrol stove than a rather strange event occurred.

Out of nowhere a Turkish Army Jeep drove into the field at speed with its two occupants waving wildly. Although these soldiers didn't appear to be at all hostile their animation was palpable as they waved their arms around and jabbered away, none of which we could comprehend. Jumping out of their Jeeps they signalled us to move and for good measure took our billy off the stove. We tried to tell them that we were quite happy in this field but this seemed to make them even more excited.

However, we packed up our belongings, closed down the stove and having been ordered to follow them we naturally complied. We managed to keep up with them for about twenty kilometres after which time they drove into another field, stopped and signalled that we could stay there for the night. Still feeling quite mystified by the turn of events we waved them 'goodbye' as they drove off.

After once again setting up camp we settled down to cook our evening meal. However whilst tucking into our supper we were startled by the noise of explosions and the sound of artillery fire as shells landed in the area we had vacated about an hour before. It then dawned on us that our previously intended camp site had been in fact the area to be used for artillery practice by the army. How lucky were we?

Next morning we enjoyed a leisurely breakfast of fresh eggs, yogurt, cheese and freshly baked bread that a little girl from a nearby farm house had brought us. We thanked her warmly and were greatly touched by such a kindly gesture.

We drove on to Agri but were still unable to find Geoff, Anne and Brian. Jack and Rob had also disappeared. However, within half an hour the whole contingent had re-formed and having compared notes we assembled and drove to within twenty-five kilometres of the Iranian border where we spent the night. We were also within sight of Mount Ararat and only eight kilometres from the Russian border. Unfortunately overnight Rob, Jack and Geoff had some belongings stolen including Geoff's boots that had been left outside his tent.

IRAN

At the time of our journey through Iran the autocratic ruler of that country was the Shah of Iran whom history would eventually reveal, ruled with an iron fist aided in no small measure by SAVAK, the dreaded Secret Police. The Shah was overthrown in a revolution inspired by Muslim clerics in 1979. However during our time there we never felt threatened and outwardly people went about their daily lives in a normal fashion. To outsiders there were no signs of political discontent.

After almost ten weeks on the road we knew that the next part of the journey would potentially be the most difficult given the distances between water replenishment stops whilst driving through the Great Sand Desert together on loosely packed unmade roads, not to mention that there would be fewer places at which we would be able to buy fresh food or vegetables.

It was therefore with some trepidation mixed with excitement that we approached the border between Turkey and Iran, eventually crossing over at the Maku checkpoint. We were given various forms to fill in but having carried out the necessary formalities we were allowed to proceed on our way.

We drove on without mishap until late afternoon when at a tea break stop Brian pointed out that one front wheel of the LVW Jeep appeared to have buckled and upon inspection we found that a couple of the bolts on the split rim had sheared. Driving very carefully we reached the town of Khvoy where we changed some currency into Iranian rials.

Walking along the streets we noticed heavily veiled heads turning our way to look at the tanned but nevertheless light coloured faces of the latest arrivals. It struck us that the townspeople seldom played host to European travellers, particularly when several of our company had blond hair, not to mention Lyn and Anne whose legs were exposed. The streets were lined with mud brick homes on whose walls tobacco leaves were laid out to dry in the sun.

We visited the local bakery where we ordered fresh bread that was specially baked for us by the local baker by placing a flattened piece of dough on the bakehouse floor where hot stones were shovelled upon them. The result after about a minute emerged as a hot dried out pancake of bread resembling a piece of chamois leather. Upon tasting the bread we later concluded that it did actually taste like chamois leather as well.

Setting up camp not far from the town we managed to insert new bolts into the wheel of the Jeep in preparation for the next day's drive.

After our overnight stay at Khvoy we made an early start for the journey to Tabriz with Jerry and Rob in the Bedford, Anne, Geoff and Brian in the RYF Jeep leaving Lyn and me in the remaining Jeep. As Lyn and I were in the leading vehicle we tried to keep the other vehicles in our sights but the unmade desert tracks were so dusty that we soon lost sight of the others. After a few kilometres we stopped in the expectation that the rest of the convoy would soon catch up. However it was a couple of hours later that they finally arrived and were told that the Bedford had sheared a bolt in its suspension. It took quite a while for us to fix the Bedford as lying under the jacked up vehicle in very high temperatures and swirling dust made repairs rather difficult to carry out.

Having resumed the day's driving it then became the turn of the LVW Jeep to give trouble when it started to lose power and the ampere meter indicated that the battery was not charging. We inspected the electrics and found that a lead to the dynamo had worked loose due to road vibration. The fault was quickly rectified.

However, our day's travails were not yet over as shortly afterwards the LVW Jeep had yet another puncture. This presented us with another problem as the spare wheel's split rim bolts had previously been damaged forcing us to cobble together another wheel. Our work on the vehicles was punctuated by showers of thick dust thrown up by the occasional passing truck that would envelop us and our vehicles.

We eventually arrived at a tiny village consisting of no more than a few mud brick huts but happily for us there was a well in the middle of the narrow main street. As we were filling up our unglazed water chatties we came across a hitch-hiker named Les Holmes. After chatting for a while we realised that he hailed from our home town of Chingford, in fact his parents' house was situated only two hundred metres from where we had lived.

By the time we had reached Tabriz the RYF Jeep and the Bedford had developed a few more problems which fortunately were able to be fixed at a local garage. Geoff's Jeep had sustained another petrol leak, an oil leak and a broken accelerator rod whilst the Bedford had been overheating due to the fierce daytime temperatures.

A mechanic inspected the Bedford and found that the radiator cap had been faulty but having fixed the problem suggested that Rob and he should shower together, an invitation which Rob hastily declined with considerable conviction.

The repairs having been carried out we headed for Teheran, Lyn having already joined Jerry and Rob whilst Brian and I followed in the LVW Jeep.

Brian and I drove for quite some time without any sign of the others but as the light was rapidly fading we decided to pull off the track, where we ate some biscuits before trying to get some sleep in the Jeep until the next morning.

Brian and I got up early (quite a relief as the Jeep was so cramped) and had a hurried breakfast intending to be on the road early. However, on pushing the Jeep's starter button there was no response from the engine, the battery having given up the ghost overnight. As we were engaged in cranking up the engine with a starting handle the rest of the party suddenly arrived. Apparently we had passed them on the road the previous night but as our headlights being so dim we had failed to see them in spite of Jerry trying to flag us down. Once again the party was together.

After eventually managing to start the Jeep we motored on to Kazimhanv where the LVW Jeep had a replacement fuel line fitted. The Iranian mechanic also pointed out that the fan belt was too long, possibly having been stretched by the prolonged heat and general wear and tear. Having installed a shorter belt the battery charged more efficiently and the engine ran cooler. The friendly mechanics also provided us with hot, black tea served with a lump of white sugar which, when placed on the tongue, allowed the tea to pass over it before the brew was consumed. It was quite refreshing. That evening we drew off the desert road to set up camp about a hundred and fifty kilometres north of Teheran.

Although we recommenced our journey early next morning we made very poor progress. The road was appalling with deep corrugations filled with dusty sand and loose sandstone chippings. Whilst the ambient temperature was well over forty degrees Celsius it did not feel unbearably harsh due to the dryness of the atmosphere. However we soon learned not to touch metallic surfaces during the heat of the day as the skin could become blistered. After covering a mere fifty kilometres we once again pulled off the track near Qasvin which was still about a hundred kilometres from Teheran.

Next morning, faced with the prospect of a further hundred kilometres on appalling roads during the heat of the day, we set off early hoping to arrive in the Iranian capital before nightfall. However, we made better progress than we had originally anticipated in fact we managed to arrive in Teheran during the afternoon. We were somewhat worried though at having lost the RYF Jeep's party en route.

As we were standing by our vehicles discussing our next move a young, well dressed Iranian man asked if he could help us. We told him we were looking for a post office and he duly directed us to one nearby. A couple of hours later we saw him again and he asked us if there was anything we particularly wished to see. At our request he took us to the nearby bazaar which was a mind boggling experience. Upon entering the huge glass roofed building we were confronted by a main thoroughfare from which numerous aisles branched out like tributaries in a complex river system. On either side of these aisles a multitude of different artificers and tradesmen jostled to show off their wares and to excitedly haggle with prospective customers.

However we were confronted everywhere by ill kempt barefoot children whose drawn and anxious faces portrayed a picture of poverty and lack of care. Our guide told us that these children were orphans who could never expect to be educated and had no prospect of improving their sorry plight. Most of these destitute children slept in the streets and carried out whatever meagre tasks they could find around the bazaar. Many were doomed to perish in the freezing winter temperatures.

Sadly all this was within a stone's throw of the splendour and opulence of the royal palace and within sight of the richest oilfields in the Middle East.

During our time with this delightful Iranian man we remarked that many young males walked hand in hand which in our culture at the time was socially unusual. He told us that in Iran, for a man and a woman to hold hands in public would be much frowned upon.

After a meal with our guide we told him that we planned to drive to Esfahan whereupon he kindly walked a considerable distance with us to our vehicles in order to indicate how to access the Esfahan road. Only after being pressed did he accept the taxi fare back to his home.

Next morning we got up at dawn and drove back towards Teheran hoping to locate Geoff, Anne and Brian but without success. Rather than hanging around hoping that they would come our way we decided to press on towards to Esfahan with the possibility of finding them en route.

What a joy it was to once again drive on tarmac roads where the smoothness of the ride appeared to have transformed the noisy, creaking Jeeps into something akin to Rolls Royce limousines. Some two hundred kilometres into the journey we came across the others and again regrouped.

The sun was really fierce during the middle of the day and after the odd tea or lunch stop, petrol tended to vaporise before reaching the Jeep's carburettors, thus starving their engines of fuel. However, when we activated the electric booster pumps the engines fired up straight away. We had been very fortunate in predicting such a contingency when preparing the Jeeps for their overland journey.

As the temperatures rose the desert seemed to become more and more forbidding and desolate with its dusty pock-marked roads and bleak sandstone mountains. That evening we camped not far from two mountains that looked quite picturesque silhouetted against the setting sun.

By now we were beginning to miss the foods to which our bodies had been accustomed over the course of our lifetime and even for those of our party who could recall the strictures of food rationing during the Second World War, our diet was becoming quite uninteresting. Fresh vegetables were becoming more and more difficult to obtain in this arid part of the world and we started to crave more interesting and nutritious fare. Even the prospect of tucking into a humble potato would have sent us into raptures. Naturally we had anticipated the gastric rigours which the desert climes would engender and had brought with us a good supply of canned and dried food which, supplemented by the local Iranian bread, provided some bulk at mealtimes. We had also brought a large quantity of rice which was becoming ever increasingly our staple diet. For years to come I for one would be left with a lasting aversion to rice as the result of overdosing on the stuff during our journey.

We had also brought with us several large containers of concentrated lime juice and at various intervals during the journey would pour water from our unglazed water chatties and mix in some lime juice as a vitamin C supplement. The chatties were invaluable during the searing desert temperatures as these unglazed clay pitchers allowed water to gradually seep though their walls thus keeping the water very cool due to process of natural evaporation. The further we drove the higher the temperatures we experienced which led us to wonder how much hotter it might become as we ventured further into the Great Sand Desert of Iran.

Not far from Esfahan we made our camp and as we had recently filled up our containers with water we decided to wash our rather sun bleached clothing and also to carry out some necessary housekeeping. Whilst I stayed in camp to check over the LVW Jeep the rest of the party drove into the nearby Murchek-Khort for a look around.

To mention the name of Esfahan had always conjured up pictures in our minds of exotic colourful mosques, magic Persian carpets and beautifully hand crafted silverware. Now we were about to find out just how accurate our mental pictures and musings had been.

As the sun appeared over the hills to our east we rose early. Once we had packed our equipment and tidied up the vehicles we planned to be on the road by 9.00 am or at least that had been our intention. However the LVW Jeep refused to start. After several turns of the starting handle we finally resorted to giving it a clutch start before it stuttered into life although it was firing on only three cylinders. We were rapidly coming to the conclusion that Willy's Jeeps did not like operating in hot weather and like recalcitrant donkeys would only move with a deal of coaxing and prodding.

Arriving at Esfahan we parked the vehicles close to a bazaar which was a veritable hive of activity.

Wherever we looked blacksmiths were making all manner of metal articles; furnaces were being fanned by small boys working the bellows, porters were frenetically rushing in all directions carrying heavy loads of materials and merchandise to various places of manufacture. The whole atmosphere was punctuated by the incessant sound of hammering as blacksmiths drew hot metal rods from their furnaces or crouched over anvils as they forged all manner of products.

The bazaars seemed endless with hundreds of small alleyways branching off from the main aisle which in turn led to a labyrinth of further stalls. Jerry was rather taken by a display of silver articles at a silversmith's workshop where, after inspecting some superb silverware he settled on two tastefully crafted matching beer mugs in solid silver. The price was seven pounds ten shillings. Strangely, although the mugs were identical, one mug cost more than the other due to the difference in the weight of silver used in its manufacture.

We had lunch at a beautifully laid out park the centre of which featured a large pool surrounded by lush green grass and trees. It was a wonderland by comparison to the dry, dusty roads over which we had driven only an hour or so before our arrival.

However, what struck us as being very strange was the sight of dozens of beautifully hand crafted carpets that were strewn willy-nilly wherever we looked with some even being left on the roads to be driven over by the few vehicles we saw. Apparently new carpets were left to weather in the sun and having been worn by constant trampling they were then taken up to the qanats situated in the hills above the town where they were washed and brought down to Esfahan again. We never ventured up into the hills to visit the qanats that were inland lakes which supplied the towns with fresh water. However, during our journey through the deserts of Iran we often came across narrow, fast running streams of cool water that had that had originated in the qanats in the hills. We were often tempted to slip into the cool, inviting water but had previously been advised that deadly snakes were also partial to a swim in the water from time to time.

After another tour of Esfahan and its main mosques we returned to our vehicles only to find that the LVW Jeep had developed yet another puncture. Once we had changed the wheel we had some difficulty in starting the engine and when it finally coughed into life it ran very badly prompting as to stop a few kilometres further on the locate the fault. We found that the distributor cam was rather worn but having reset the ignition points the Jeep recovered quite well and we were able to reach Khurman, twenty kilometres south of Esfahan where we camped overnight.

The fourteenth of September was another day we would never be able to forget. After an early morning start we continued our drive along the dusty unmade road in fierce temperatures for another six hours when suddenly we heard a loud BANG! The Bedford slowly ground to a halt. Upon inspection we found that the timing chain had jammed and broken, also shattering the timing chain housing and the camshaft.

Geoff and I stripped the engine down and removed the timing chain housing and also the broken camshaft. Removal of the camshaft proved to be very difficult as the steel wishbone holding the front suspension prevented us from removing the entire crank case cover in fact we had to extricate the camshaft from the cam followers by feeling where they were. The sweltering heat and swirling desert dust added considerably to our discomfort.

We then had a discussion and it was decided that a Jeep would take the broken parts to the nearest town of Abadeh in the hope of obtaining another camshaft and timing housing although we were not very optimistic.

The following day Geoff, Rob and Jerry drove to Abedeh but were advised that our only chance of obtaining replacement parts would be back in Esfahan.

It took several hours to drive all the way back to Esfahan but upon our arrival Geoff became violently ill with diarrhoea and vomiting. Shortly afterwards I also started to suffer from the same illness which then left just Jerry and Rob to go in search of a replacement camshaft. As luck would have it, Jerry came across a Vauxhall Victor taxi cab and knowing that it would have been made in England by the same company that manufactured the Bedford van, he asked the cab driver through an interpreter where he would be likely to obtain spares for the stricken vehicle. The taxi driver directed them to the local Esfahan motor vehicle breakers yard.

The owner of the breakers yard pointed to a mountain of engine parts and also a pile consisting of old crankshafts and camshafts. Miraculously they found what they were looking for. Although he would normally have sold much of his stock merely as scrap metal he obviously knew that they were desperate and charged seven pounds for this rusty piece of metal. They had no option but to pay up and return to our Jeep. All we needed now was a new timing chain complete with the chain tensioner and in addition, some work done on the battered timing chain case. Fortunately a motor mechanic was able to make up the parts we required and another mechanic placed the damaged timing chain case into a furnace and welded it back into its original shape.

By the time they returned to the Jeep, Geoff was feeling less ill and was not vomiting, presumably because he had nothing left inside him. However, as I still had a severe case of the squitters, we decided that I should drive the Jeep as I would be able to stop whenever the need arose, which was very, very frequently. Fortunately for us we carried a generous supply of water in locally made 'chatties' which did at least enable us to remain hydrated after such punishing diarrhoea.

What a great relief it was to arrive back at camp later that evening

The following day work on the Bedford commenced although I remained in bed for a while whilst sporadically running out into the desert to relieve myself or to vomit. Work on the Bedford took the whole day, our progress being hampered by our inability to see most of the camshaft followers which were hidden from view at the base of the engine. Guiding them into position by 'feel' was very tricky.

Finally, the job was finished but we decided not to start the engine until the following day as darkness was rapidly approaching.

The next day, with feelings of optimism tinctured by not a little trepidation, we turned the key of the Bedford but it wouldn't start. We checked and rechecked every aspect of our work but could not get the engine to fire. We removed spark plugs, placed fingers down the plug apertures in order to feel the pistons come up to 'top dead centre' and again checked the engine timing but all to no avail. We took the timing case cover off, checked that the timing 'dots' were correctly aligned but still it wouldn't respond.

Finally, it was decided that Geoff would tow Jerry and Rob in the Bedford to nearby Abadeh where it was hoped they would find a motor mechanic. Upon making enquiries they were told that there was only one motor mechanic in the town but that he was in bed and dying. However a local Iranian took them to the man's house and although looking very frail he got up from his sick bed and agreed to help. He took out a spark plug, put his finger down into a cylinder, brought the piston up to 'top dead centre' and then inspected the timing chain. He found that although the camshaft we had obtained was identical to the Bedford part, it was actually from a Vauxhall Victor car where the timing dot aligning the firing of the pistons was in a different position. After making the adjustment the Bedford roared into life. However although the Bedford rose up like Lazarus they feared that the very accommodating mechanic would not be so fortunate. Jerry had very little money with him but the mechanic was happy to receive a pound note and a packet of biscuits for his labours.

When Rob and Jerry brought back the Bedford under its own power we were overjoyed. Having given the vehicle another inspection we found that the sump was leaking oil which necessitated tightening up the sump bolts. Fortunately this cured the problem.

It was great to be on the road again as we drove towards Abadeh where we filled up with petrol as well as taking the opportunity to replenish our supply of water, carefully dropping two water purifying tablets into the chatties as usual.

The tarmac road surface out of Abadeh was most welcome but having left the town we were again confronted by the usual dusty desert roads as we branched off towards Kerman. After the worries of the preceding few days, not to mention the painful stomach upsets, we decided to set up camp early to enjoy a much needed rest.

The following day was the 20th September and although we had become quite used to the atrocious roads and long periods of isolation, the next few hours tended to reinforce feelings of apprehension particularly when we arrived at a fork in the dusty desert track. We stopped the vehicles and the whole party got out and stared at the fork in the track and asked Rob the navigator, which one we should take.

After studying the map and checking the compass he signified that we should take the left fork, adding that it would be another five hundred kilometres of desert tracks before we would reach Kerman. The prospect seemed quite daunting, not only because there were no signposts for confirmation of our whereabouts but because the road was really only a narrow, corrugated track set in the most desolate countryside. There was not even the hint of a tree or shrub to break up the arid scene confronting our party.

Conversation in the Jeeps was impossible as the vehicles lurched from side to side on the corrugations and the dust thrown up by the Bedford in front restricted our vision to a few metres. When we finally stopped for the day we had covered only two hundred and fifty kilometres. Unfortunately the dreadful condition of the track had thrown the LVW Jeep around so much that we had lost a four gallon can of water and a bucket overboard. Also our earthenware water chatty had been smashed. The loss of the chatty was particularly unfortunate as we had relied on it to keep our water cool during the heat of the day. However, as we were unable to replace it at the time, we poured some of our precious water supply into a plastic container around which we had wrapped a wet towel allowing the water to keep cool by the process of natural evaporation.

By evening we were more than relieved to get out of the vehicles and set up camp in the desert. The area in which we were camped was a totally desolate place. The feeling of desolation was so complete that it seemed to exude a rather eerie atmosphere.

After a meal and with very little else to occupy us, Brian and I decided to take a walk across the sand. The sun having set, the heat of the day had given way to almost freezing temperatures with no cloud in the sky to conserve the heat. However after a brisk walk of about two kilometres we stopped to admire the full moon and total stillness of this most desolate part of the world. However, shortly after stopping we heard a distant sound and wondered what it could be. As the sound became louder we recognised the noise to be that of a steady drum beat. Out of the darkness some fifty metres away we saw a camel train of thirteen camels linked nose to tail as they trudged through the desert accompanied by the camel driver beating time on his drum at the rear of the procession. We crouched down wishing to savour the moment without the camel driver seeing us. He was oblivious to our presence as Brian and I crouched there, transfixed by the scene out of a childhood picture book.

The next morning we experienced another most unusual phenomenon. Never before had we been in any part of the world where nothing could be seen from one horizon to the other. Not a tree, shrub, road, mountain, house nor any human being except for our own company. As we cast our eyes over this desolate landscape we felt as though we had been suddenly dropped onto another planet. All we were able to see was the curvature of the earth in every direction. We were indeed standing on top of the world.

However, there were times when in spite of our total isolation we were confronted by the odd surprise. One morning, in the middle of nowhere, we awoke to be greeted by the sight of a number of vultures circling our encampment. At the time I was reminded of a line in Winston Churchill's book 'My early Life' when, during the Boer War, he was hiding from the enemy in a wood "where my only companion was a vulture which took an extravagant interest in my wellbeing".

Fortunately for us, we were aware that vultures only consume carrion and are not attracted to live flesh.

We again made an early start in order to make as many kilometres as possible before the sun became more intense but no sooner had we got under way than the wheel on Geoff's Jeep came off. He had apparently forgotten to tighten the wheel nuts after repairing a puncture the previous evening. The desert track was very punishing not only to the vehicles but also to their occupants, particularly to those of us driving the Jeeps. The leaf springs offered a very hard ride and as the petrol tank was situated under the driver's seat, one's backside became quite numb and sore the further the journey progressed.

As we were approaching Kerman the dull flat landscape gave way to distant mountains on either side of the track. However as Jack and I peered through the Jeep's windscreen we both remarked how strange it was to see a huge beach leading down to the sea where gentle waves rippled on the shore. Knowing that we were nowhere near to a sea we nevertheless became quite excited until it dawned on us that this was in fact just a mirage. There was neither beach nor water but only kilometres of sand as far as the eye could see with the heat above the road surface creating the shimmering mirage towards which we were driving.

It was a relief to arrive in Kerman where we wasted no time in finding a police station in order to have our visas extended, our mechanical troubles having unexpectedly delayed our journey through Iran. We also found a motor mechanic who was able to weld the chassis of the RYF Jeep which had sustained some damage from the desert corrugations.

After a most productive afternoon in Kerman we moved on towards Bam. Although the roads were still very poor and in some places rose up and down like a scenic railway we nevertheless made good time and were able to set up our evening camp and prepare our evening meal without the usual rush.

It was now the 23rd September and with the vehicles running well we set our sights on reaching Bam before lunchtime, in fact we covered the one hundred and eighty kilometres without incident, arriving in Bam by early afternoon where we stopped at a local service station for petrol. Refuelling vehicles in such remote places was always a tedious affair. Each gallon of petrol had to be pumped manually from an underground tank until it filled a glass cylinder designed to hold just one gallon of fuel which was then released into the vehicle's petrol tank. Having deposited one gallon the process was repeated until the vehicle's petrol tank had been filled. This meant that we had to record the exact number of gallons pumped each time we refuelled the vehicles.

At this particular service station the owner tried to charge us for more petrol than the vehicles' actual tank capacity. The argument became very heated to the point where the attendant tried to snatch the keys of the Bedford whereupon Rob grabbed him roughly by the shirt. This infuriated the garage owner even more. We therefore threw the correct money onto the ground and drove off, leaving the owner shaking his fist.

As Bam was renowned for the succulence of its dates, we stopped at a property and purchased a box which we ate together with a cup of soup. However, just as we were saying how tasty the dates were, a fierce wind sprang up whisking the soup out of our cups and peppering the dates with desert sand.

From Bam onwards the roads deteriorated even further, with the corrugations becoming even deeper with every kilometre covered. Conversation was impossible as we peered through the dust laden windscreens. The ride was so uncomfortable it felt as though the Jeep's springs had been removed and had been replaced by a set of pneumatic drills. After two hundred and fifty kilometres our hips and backs were given some respite from the rigours of the day's journey as we camped in the desert overnight.

Following the discomfort of a day's driving, often under difficult conditions, it was always a pleasure to have our evening meal and then curl up in our sleeping bags and admire the stars. At such times I would often to lose myself in a book, reading by the light of a six volt globe attached to the battery of the Jeep. It seemed an odd place in which to read an English novel but being a lover of Charles Dickens' novels I managed to read 'Nicholas Nickleby'. After travelling back in time to nineteenth century Britain and reading about the cruelty to children described within its pages it seemed strange to emerge once more into the real world of the twentieth century, lying in the desert in one of the remotest places on the planet.

Next day, whilst driving in the LVW Jeep with Brian we were confronted by sand dunes on either side of the track that eventually led to rugged rock formations. The atrocious road conditions continued to take their toll on the vehicles. The Jeep in which we were travelling started to overheat and the radiator began to emit steam. Fortunately we did not lose too much water as, prior to the journey, we had fitted a tube to the radiator overflow pipe which was in turn connected to a one gallon metal tank lashed to the front bumper bar. Thus, steam from the radiator found its way into the holding tank where it condensed back into water. We did manage to make a temporary repair to the radiator which held together until the evening.

Just before nightfall we reached the outskirts of Zahedan where we managed to find a valley that was well sheltered from the wind and an ideal place in which to set up our camp for the night.

Driving into Zahedan the next morning we were hoping to purchase some fresh vegetables but unfortunately all the shops and businesses were closed. By this time our visas had almost run out again but fortunately for us the local tourist office was able to oblige and having given them our particulars we were asked to come back later.

This interval allowed us to survey the town. The local inhabitants looked quite different from the Iranians we had previously seen. Their complexions were darker and they dressed more like Indians with the men wearing turbans instead of the traditional Arab fez. Most of the locals appeared to be very poor; there were beggars everywhere. In a gutter I even saw a dead child but by the time we returned that way the child had been removed. It was a very sad spectacle indeed, in fact we were glad to pick up our documentation and make for the Pakistani border at Mirajavea.

On arrival at the border checkpoint we were warned that it would be safer to remain in their courtyard overnight. Apparently the area was known to harbour bandits and other lawless bands of men so we readily took their advice. The area in which the checkpoint was located must once have been an ancient fort which to us appeared to resemble the headquarters of the French Foreign Legion or the place in which Beau Geste had once been billeted with its high solid stone walls and parapets. Access to the courtyard was gained not over a moat and drawbridge but through a heavily timbered gate that was securely locked and barred at night.

The man in charge of Customs did not seem at all happy and by the look of his swollen face was apparently suffering the effects of a toothache. Brian questioned the man as best he could which confirmed that this was the case. Brian then produced a roll of dental tools and suggested that he extract the offending molar. The Customs man appeared amazed at this sudden turn of events and readily agreed to the procedure.

Thus, in his tiny office with an audience consisting of a little boy, seven European travellers and a couple of curious locals Brian applied a local anaesthetic and extracted the troublesome tooth. I am sure that had the patient been a devout Muslim his confidence in Allah would have been much enhanced by the evening's proceedings.

After a meal and a walk within the safe confines of the fort we crawled into our sleeping bags and went to sleep.

WEST PAKISTAN

When we undertook this journey almost fifty years ago Pakistan comprised two separate and far removed states, namely West Pakistan and East Pakistan following independence from Great Britain in August, 1947. However in 1971 the two Pakistani states became separate sovereign nations and as a consequence West Pakistan became known as just Pakistan and East Pakistan became an independent state to be known as Bangladesh.

When we crossed the border from Iran we were once again required to drive on the left hand side of the road. However this didn't make much difference at the time as the road on which we were travelling was still only a sandy desert track, a situation to which we had become accustomed over the last several thousand kilometres. Two things we did observe were that the few people we encountered possessed darker complexions to people in Iran and the men usually wore turbans.

After driving for a few hours the road surfaces became even more treacherous. Loose sandy areas became more numerous and in some parts sand dunes had spilled out onto the road adding yet another hazard to the already difficult driving conditions. Although we managed to avoid the more conspicuous sandy parts we were still apt to be caught unawares. On one occasion the LVW Jeep became stuck in a sand drift and it took some considerable time to dig the sand away from the wheels before being able to extricate the vehicle using a combination of four wheel drive and booster gears.

It had now been three months since leaving England and some tensions amongst the participants were now starting to emerge. The original intention of the party was to travel to Kathmandu, sell the vehicles there and then use local transport from Kathmandu to Singapore in order to catch flights to Australia. However, Geoff and Anne had now decided upon alternative arrangements although still intending to finally reach Sydney where Geoff had secured lucrative employment with a local company. Additionally Brian had decided that instead of travelling for another two or three months within Asia he would reach Delhi then find his way back to England from there. Presumably he was missing his fiancée as well as his family. However, before the two parties split up we arranged to all meet in Quetta to tidy up financial arrangements.

Our group of Jerry, Rob, Lyn, Jack and I took the Bedford and LVW Jeep and set off on the road bound for Quetta some five hundred kilometres away. After a hundred and fifty kilometre drive we found a suitable camp site just off the desert track close to the village of Yakmach where we spent the night.

Shortly after resuming our journey the following day the Jeep came to a sudden stop and when we lifted the vehicle's bonnet the cause of the problem became obvious. The battery had split in two, doubtless due to the stresses and strains imposed upon it by prolonged heat and the rough desert tracks. This was a real blow to our plans as we were still three hundred and fifty kilometres from Quetta, the only town with a prospect of our purchasing a replacement battery.

At that time we had been hopeful that the occupants of the RYF Jeep might catch up with us on their way to Quetta but unfortunately we saw no sign of them. It was therefore decided that we had no option than to harness up the Bedford to tow the stricken Jeep.

The Bedford's small 1500cc engine laboured valiantly as it towed the heavy Jeep for over two hundred kilometres until the Bedford's engine suddenly gave up the ghost about fifteen kilometres from the village of Nushki.

Being stranded on a remote desert track with two broken down vehicles was quite a worrying experience. Had we been able to transfer the Bedford's battery to the Jeep, we could have arranged for the Jeep to tow the lighter vehicle. However the batteries on both vehicles were of different voltages. We therefore had no alternative but to get the Bedford mobile again.

We crawled under the van and eventually traced the trouble to a locking pin on the petrol pump which having worked loose had caused the pump's arm to drop into the vehicle's sump. Removal of the vehicle's sump was a very messy business but we were finally able to retrieve the arm and fit a replacement fuel pump from our box of spares. Once more the Bedford rose again.

Having surveyed the hilly terrain towards Quetta we decided that the Bedford did not possess the necessary power to tow the Jeep over such undulating territory. Therefore it was decided that Jerry, Rob and Lyn would drive the Bedford to Quetta leaving Jack and me in the desert with the Jeep. In the meantime Jerry would purchase a replacement battery in Quetta and drive back the following day.

Jack and I waved 'goodbye' to the others as they drove off and we settled down for a long wait until Jerry's eventual return, hopefully bringing with him the six volt battery required for the Jeep.

The area in which we were marooned was as desolate as any place we had previously encountered. There was not even a tree or shrub in sight and no sign of animal or birdlife at all, our only companions being squadrons of tenacious flies that constantly buzzed around our faces. With no trees or bushes to afford us shade we sought sanctuary under the Jeep having first wrapped ourselves in mosquito nets. At last the sun slipped over the horizon and we were able to emerge from under the Jeep and gulp in the cool night air.

Unfortunately our supply of drinking water had now become very low compelling us to economise consumption particularly as we were unsure as to when Jerry would return. We also felt it unwise to eat any of our dehydrated food as this would have exacerbated our thirsts, but at least there was some comfort in being able to breathe in the refreshing breeze that had sprung up following the sunset. Jack and I must have presented a somewhat forlorn picture as we sat by the side of the Jeep, our only light being that of a candle we had placed in an empty pickle jar to protect it from the evening breeze.

Just prior to crawling into the Jeep for the night, a truck emerged from the track and seeing our plight, two Pakistani men dropped a couple of water melons in the sand close to where were sitting. We could not believe our luck and yelled our thanks as their truck departed the scene. It took us little time to scrape the juice from one of the melons after deciding to save the second one for the next day. The sensation of the sweet liquid drizzling down our throats was pure nectar. Further into our journey through Pakistan we were to find that everywhere we travelled the local people were the essence of kindness itself.

After a restless night cooped up in the Jeep and shrouded under mosquito nets we emerged feeling very thirsty and in need of a good meal. By that time our supply of drinking water had become a real cause for concern so we turned to the remaining water melon to assuage our thirst and provide some food as well.

The morning was again spent underneath the Jeep trying to evade the flies that buzzed around us in droves. We dug a hole in a nearby dried up river bed but even a metre below the surface there was no sign of water. Although we knew that we could not drink the water from the Jeep's radiator, we drained off a cupful with which to wash our grimy hands but this resulted in them smelling of oil.

There was little we could do but wait. Jack wandered around with a towel draped over his head looking for all-the-world like a latter day Lawrence of Arabia. At one point he beckoned to me and asked if I could see a lake some distance away. Strangely, I saw it too with the rays of the sun shimmering off the water and trees on its banks. Although only a tantalising mirage it nevertheless looked real and deliciously inviting.

Late in the afternoon Jerry arrived with a second-hand six volt battery he had purchased in Quetta. However, he hadn't brought any water with him. We quickly installed the battery and pushed the Jeep's starter button. Although the engine turned over we were unable to start the motor. We tested all ignition systems and finally traced the problem to the coil. Fortunately we were carrying a spare coil which we fitted but still the Jeep refused to start. Upon further inspection we found that a tiny beryllium contact in the distributor had sheared off.

Once again fortune was on our side as we found that we were carrying a spare distributor in our spares box. We wasted no time in extracting the contact from the spare distributor but having installed it, the Jeep's engine still refused to start. By now the replacement battery was unable to turn over the engine so we resorted to using the starting handle. Even then the engine refused to fire.

Feeling tired, thirsty and rather grumpy we placed Jack into the driver's seat whilst Jerry and I pushed the Jeep up an escarpment and shoved it down the hill. The engine to our great relief finally burst into life. We were now on our way to Quetta.

After about fifteen kilometres we came across a lone house and decided to ask the owner for some water. The Sikh owner must have been a person of some substance as, whilst walking up the path to his house we came across a small pool fed from a clear spring. Upon asking the owner for water he told us that the water in the pool was pure and that we could help ourselves. We sank our mugs into the water and savoured the moment as the cool, clear water washed down our throats. Never had a drink tasted as refreshing as the water from that spring.

By early evening we eventually arrived in Quetta where Jerry, Rob and Lyn had secured accommodation in a Dak Bungalow. After lying under a Jeep for almost two days we were now looking forward to the pleasurable prospect of sleeping in a permanent structure for the first time in over three months.

After a cold bath taken in a rather rudimentary ablutions outhouse we tucked into a magnificent pot of stew cooked up by Lyn. What a luxury it was to retire with a full belly to the comfort of a real bed safe in the knowledge that we would be staying in Quetta for at least until the others had arrived which as it turned out would be a few days hence.

Dak Bungalow was the name originally given to a house used by travellers along the old Dak routes in India during colonial times and is sometimes referred to in some of Rudyard Kipling's tales. The European equivalent would have been Youth Hostels in that they were rustic in appearance whilst supplying the basic needs of travellers and wayfarers.

The bungalow in which we were housed was decidedly Victorian in appearance and having been whitewashed many years before was now displaying a rather tired and somewhat worn appearance. The ablutions area certainly dated back to the times of the Raj, being equipped with an ancient galvanized iron hip bath requiring the user to sit upright in the tub and lather up with soap before pouring pitchers of water over his or her body. The lavatory was also a study of antiquity. It consisted of two bricks placed on the concrete floor upon which one squatted to do the business. Each day the height of the excrement would increase until being removed at the weekend. At the beginning of the week it was quite easy to balance on just two bricks, indeed it was possible for the user to hyperventilate, do the business and leave without taking an extra breath. However, balancing on three or four bricks at the end of the week became a rather challenging operation, not to mention the overpowering stench which by then was permeating the area.

The last day of September duly arrived as did Geoff, Anne and Brian in the RYF Jeep in the late afternoon. They had apparently experienced an even more torrid time than us. Their Jeep had suffered so many punctures along the way that a couple of inner tubes had been damaged beyond repair forcing them to stuff the tyres with clothing and towels to enable them to complete the journey to Quetta.

After an evening meal we discussed the allocation of the remaining funds before retiring to bed.

The following day the manager of the bungalow was able to provide breakfast for two shillings each person. We enjoyed this sumptuous meal before taking our first trip into the town of Quetta.

Quetta was a fascinating place, one noticeable aspect being that there were very few motor cars on the streets, the main modes of transport being bicycles, scooter rickshaws and even Hansom cabs. There was also a marked British influence not only in the streets but in the shops as well with advertising hoardings in English extolling the virtues of British products as well as local goods. Women were heavily veiled suggesting the overall influence of the Muslim culture. As a tyre from the Bedford was in need of repair Jerry and I drove it to a nearby motor vehicle repair shop where the mechanic vulcanized a new nozzle onto the inner tube and having taken great care over his work refused to charge us explaining that their religion had taught them to be hospitable to strangers. Whilst this work was being carried out a Pakistani radio technician fell into conversation with us and invited us out for morning tea. It was a joy to tuck into sandwiches made with fresh English style white bread together with cups of local tea.

We were most impressed by people's hospitality and friendliness. Speaking to Geoff later in the day he told us that he had had a similar experience with welders who had carried out a complex welding job on his Jeep's chassis and yet had refused payment.

In the evening I went for a walk with Brian. After a while we found ourselves in the slum quarters of the town with its run down houses and squalid workshops where men were still working at benches and lathes. The area was reeking with the odour of open sewers and in the small cafes meals were being served. We also came upon a cul-de-sac at the end of which was a timber stage upon which several unveiled and attractive looking girls were seated. The spectre of two blond European men evoked curiosity bordering on excitement not just from the girls but also from a man who was presumably their minder. He tried to coax us into the building but we both scurried off and into the night.

The first of October had been quite successful. We had sorted out the finances and separated the items of camping gear which were no longer required. As luck would have it, the son of a nomadic tribal chief arrived in the forecourt of the bungalow and asked if we wished to sell any of our equipment. As Rob had no further use for his tent he showed it to the man. It was an 'igloo' tent equipped with a frame held in place by a pneumatic superstructure that was inflated by the use of a car tyre pump. Unfortunately it possessed a predilection to collapsing a few hours after being erected. We were apprehensive lest the chief's son use it straight away and come looking for us the following day. The chief's son seemed to be fascinated by Jerry's electric shaver and was delighted when Jerry sold it to him for a few rupees.

The following day we rose before dawn and were packed and on our way by 6.30a.m. The early morning was extremely cold as we drove through the town past people making their way to work with scarves muffled around their necks or blankets draped around their shoulders, their expended breath lingering on the cold morning air as they hurried along.

We motored on and watched the sun rise over the horizon. It was quite a relief as we gradually reduced altitude and descended into warmer temperatures. On countless occasions we came across nomadic tribes leading heavily laden camels and asses. We even noticed chickens in wicker cages that had been tied onto the backs of donkeys plus many children and dogs that scampered in and out of the processions.

At Jacobabad we filled up with petrol and as we were doing so the proprietor sent his boy out to buy bottles of Coca Cola for us. We enjoyed these as we sat under a ceiling fan in his office.

For the next eighty kilometres prior to reaching Sukhat the roads deteriorated, slowing our progress. By the time we arrived there it was too late to find a Dak Bungalow. However, we decided to set up camp amidst huge palm trees on the banks of the Indus River. We took little time in erecting our mosquito nets and having done so shoved our sleeping bags under the nets ready to enjoy a night's sleep under the stars. The sunset was the most beautiful I had ever experienced in my life. It was as though an artist had run riot across the sky with a large brush charged with vermilion paint before adding palm trees into the foreground as an afterthought.

The place in which I had chosen to sleep was some distance from where the others were camped and having snuggled up in my sleeping bag I gazed at the superb night sky before dozing off to sleep.

I awoke at dawn with a start. Looking down on me was a small boy accompanied by his dog and three large water buffalo, one of which was slobbering over the mosquito net under which I was lying. As the sun was rising, several very attractive young women wearing brightly coloured dresses appeared on the scene, walking towards a nearby well with earthenware chatties balanced on their heads. They were very much surprised at the sight of a European body emerging from beneath a mosquito net and chatted excitedly at this unusual spectacle.

Once we had repaired the Jeep's radiator and fixed a faulty fuel pump we quit the camp site and headed for Multan. On the way we were delayed by the passing of a train through a level crossing. Whilst we were waiting, the level crossing keeper invited us into his cabin for a cup of tea. We were quite sorry when the ancient steam train has passed through and it had become time to leave this very hospitable Pakistani.

By evening we were still over a hundred and thirty kilometres from Multan so we decided to stay at a guest house called Guest House No 2 where we were served a delicious curry for dinner. The brick building may well have dated back to colonial times with its regal arches and whitewashed walls that gave it a rather sanitized appearance.

Just before 'lights out' a strange creature flew into the room that Rob, Jack and I were sharing. It was bright green in colour with antenna and mandibles, its appearance resembling the cross between a bat, a grasshopper and a frog. We summoned the person in charge who calmly removed his turban and dropped it onto the creature before releasing it into the night air. In retrospect we thought it might have been a rather well fed locust.

The day's journey was delayed for a couple of hours as the Bedford needed some minor repairs to be carried out. There was a problem with the fuel pump, the steering arm was broken and the accelerator arm had seized. However we were on the road by midday but after about only fifty kilometres over very rough roads the Jeep hit a deep pothole causing a leaf in the rear spring to break. However as the vehicle was still driveable we decided to continue our journey to Multan and hopefully have the repair done there.

The road on which we were driving was elevated with rice paddies on either side below road level. When we stopped for a break to stretch our legs we decided to take a look at these irrigated fields and noticed that small fish actually inhabited the channels between the crops of rice.

When we reached Multan we immediately took the Jeep to a mechanic for repair and whilst this was being done took advantage of the time to look around. By now we were sporting very long hair, much bleached by the sun and in fact we were looking generally rather scruffy and in need of a haircut.

Rob and I came across a barber's shop but as it was in total darkness we started to move away assuming that it was closed. However, the owner came out and told us that they were experiencing some trouble with the lighting but were still open for business.

After candles had been lit we ensconced ourselves in the chairs and were immediately asked if we wanted either Coke or Fanta. We were quite mystified and explained that we had really come in for just a haircut, only to be told by the proprietor that refreshments were always offered to their customers. Two Cokes were sent for and soon we were having several weeks of hair shorn from our heads whilst drinking cool bottles of Coca Cola. Whilst having our haircuts a young boy fanned us, just as punkah wallahs would have done in colonial times. Finally the hairdressers introduced us to their 'piece de resistance' in the form of a scalp massage carried out with much vigour before withdrawing the sheets from our shoulders and announcing that the total charge amounted to one rupee each, the Coke having been 'on the house'.

Meanwhile Jerry, Lyn and Jack had met a medical student from Niarobi who invited us all for coffee in a nearby hostel for students. Luli was a most amiable person with a keen sense of humour. He gave us many tips about living in Pakistan and showed us around the local hospital in Multan. The hospital was located in five hundred acres of beautifully laid out gardens and could accommodate six hundred in-patients.

After farewelling Luli we drove about fifteen kilometres to the outskirts of Lahore where we again camped under the stars.

Next day, the fifth of October we made an early start hoping to reach Lahore within a couple of hours but soon found that the Bedford was running badly. There was a whining noise coming from the engine accompanied by an occasional clattering sound and the battery was not charging. For some time I had suspected that the dynamo had not been charging to full capacity and when we dismantled the dynamo we found that its commutator winding, bronze bearings and carbon brushes were badly worn. We managed to rebuild it from spare parts and after reinstalling the dynamo the vehicle ran well and the battery began to charge again.

Just prior to our arrival into Lahore we unexpectedly ran into a dip in the road large enough to submerge our vehicles' wheels in water that penetrated their distributors causing both vehicles to stop dead in midstream. After a great effort we were able to manhandle them out of the water before opening the bonnets and allowing the heat of the sun to dry out the sodden distributors. The remainder of the journey was not without incident either as we came across a wake of vultures tearing at the carcass of a camel that had obviously died overnight. We immediately stopped the vehicles and grabbing our cine cameras, started filming, hoping to capture them on film as they took to the air. We threw stones at them to encourage them to fly until it dawned on us that they had gorged themselves to such an extent that were unable to take off.

Upon reaching Lahore we located an American Express Office but it was closed. However, as we were walking away from the office we met a couple of Germans who told us that they were going to the nearest Youth Hostel and that we could follow them in our vehicles. Not long after setting out we lost sight of them and became totally lost ourselves, in fact we ended up in a narrow lane just wide enough to accommodate a vehicle. Unfortunately the lane became narrower and narrower as it led to a bazaar but we were unable to either back the vehicles or to turn them around. Incredulous stall holders shifted their barrows, others rushed to retrieve their bikes before we ran over them and shoppers scattered as we ploughed our way up alleyways with overhanging bolts of cloth brushing the tops of our vehicles. Excited Pakistanis gaped at us as small boys deposited useful items such as rotten apples and cabbages into our open vehicles. Finally we found our way through this living hell feeling as though we had been the prime characters in a grisly nightmare.

Eventually we found the Hostel and having installed ourselves there had a shower and went to bed. We never did see the Germans again.

During the journey it had always been a joy to pick up our mail from local American Express Offices and also to post our own letters back to family and friends at home. We also took the opportunity to send spools of 35mm still and 8mm movie films home for Dad to process. Viewing the films also gave our families some idea of our experiences in pictorial form. However, this was not without its unforeseen consequences.

Jerry had arranged with our father to send his 8mm cine films back to England together with appropriate descriptions of the images shown. Dad was very enthusiastic about the arrangement as, after having had them developed he could join the films together to show them at an 'Old People's Fellowship' meeting at the local Methodist church.

However, on one such occasion, having joined several spools of film together he omitted to vet their contents beforehand. Unbeknown to him, Jerry had taken a shot of a naked Jack far off in the desert as he inspected a painful heat rash. Picking his moment, Jerry zoomed in just as Jack was bathing his rather sore scrotum and gonads with cool water.

Dad was not amused at the time but in later years admitted that it had been quite a coup. Doubtless the old dears would have been given the thrill of a lifetime but I am unsure as to Dad's reaction had he been requested by one of the old ladies for a re-run of that particular film clip.

After collecting our mail we took a Hansom cab to the Lahore Zoo before driving to the beautiful Shalimar Gardens where we relaxed over tea and cakes.

In the evening we made our way to 'Lords', which seemed to be a very upmarket restaurant to us. It apparently dated back to the days of the Raj and in fact the old brick building may well have been a gentlemen's club during that era. We ate in style and treated our stomachs to gastronomic delights about which we had been fantasising for several months. Our meal included prawn cocktail to start, then tornado steak with grilled mushrooms, spinach, cauliflower and chips followed by egg custard and cream to round off the meal. It was truly wonderful to indulge in such a scrumptious meal especially as there wasn't a grain of rice in sight. The bill came to ten shillings each including what was probably a generous tip. The excellent waiter must have been very surprised at the size of the tip we gave him as he repeated "Very, very thankyou Sahib". It really brought home to us how lowly paid some of the local people must have been and how fortunate we were to have been born in the comparatively richer western world.

Lahore possessed a wonderful atmosphere. Many of the different cultures over the years had melded it into what had become a truly beautiful city where motor cars, Hansom cabs, motor scooters and bicycles seemed able to dwell in inconspicuous harmony with the nomadic cattle that roamed the various areas of that city's greenbelt. But most of all we enjoyed our time roaming around the Shalimar Gardens and the friendly people with whom it had been our pleasure to have encountered.

Two days later we left Lahore and drove

straight towards West Pakistan's border with India. Our eleven day sojourn in West Pakistan had been one of great enjoyment and we were very grateful in being able to leave that country with such wonderful memories. Never once did we experience any hostility or harsh words; on the contrary everyone with whom we had been in contact had been kind, helpful and generous to a fault and ever ready to go that extra mile in order to help make our stay in their country an enjoyable experience. They certainly managed to do that in good measure. We held out hopes that in India we would experience a similar warmth and generosity of spirit.

INDIA

The formalities at the border took an inordinately long time but having finally completed the necessary documentation we drove on towards Amritsar. Once there we found the streets thronged with thousands of people and a preponderance of bicycles, tricycles, scooter cabs and rickshaws vying for space on roads already choked by pedestrians who contributed to the atmosphere of utter confusion. Women (unveiled) many of whom were riding bikes, were dressed in gaily coloured saris that complemented their dark complexions and finely chiselled features.

On the opposite side of the lake we viewed the famous Golden Temple of Amritsar. However, as the scene was one of overpopulated confusion we felt uncomfortable about leaving the vehicles in the midst of the throng. We therefore decided to make for Delhi without delay.

We drove along tarmac roads lined with superb avenues of green trees until we found a suitable site on which to camp. We had covered over a hundred and fifty kilometres since setting out that morning and after ensconcing ourselves in a wooded area a Sikh gentleman appeared and welcomed us to his land. He also showed interest in our planned travels and asked if he could be of any assistance.

Next morning we repaired another puncture in the Jeep after which we tried without success to start its engine. It took little time to locate the problem and after adjusting the distributor's points with feeler gauges we were on our way. The roadside was very green which made a welcome change from the desert wastes of Iran and much of West Pakistan which suggested that the area in which we now found ourselves had recently received quite heavy rain.

We reached Delhi in the early evening and approaching from the east came across streets thronged with people, scooters, scooter taxis, rickshaws and bikes. One area through which we passed was home to hundreds of poverty stricken people living on waste land and cooking over smoky open fires. The adults were ill clad and many of the children were running around not only barefoot but naked as well.

Having arrived in Delhi it took us a long time to locate the American Express Office and an even longer time to find the hostel where we had planned to stay, finally arriving well after nightfall. The hostel was located within sight of the Qutab Minar Tower which bore a marked resemblance to the well known Monument Tower in London. However the Qutab Minar had been erected some five hundred years before Christopher Wren's Tower which had been built as a monument to the 1666 Great Fire of London.

The hostel was austere to say the least, bereft even of basic amenities such as electricity or bathing and toilet facilities. However we soon managed to rig up a light having brought the Jeep's battery into our sleeping quarters. The person running the hostel showed us around our rather monastic room before advising us about the outside toilet that was situated in the garden about twenty

metres at the end of an overgrown path. She warned us that the gardens were infested with deadly cobras and suggested that if we needed to go to the toilet after dark, we should bang a wooden staff on the ground and swing a kerosene lantern about to ward off the snakes. She then produced a staff and an antiquated lantern before leaving us for the night. Needless to say, none of our company dared to venture out that night. As we were billeted on an open ground floor veranda, we were able to take the opportunity to pee over the parapet before crawling into bed for the night.

The following day we drove downtown into Delhi to pick up our mail from the American Express Office and thence to the Nepalese Embassy to enquire about visas required for our stay in Kathmandu. We were very disappointed to learn that within thirty minutes the embassy would be closing for a period of eleven days. However, after advising them that we couldn't to wait until then to obtain our visas, they agreed to open the office in two days time when the visas would be ready.

We also called at the bank where we had previously arranged for British money to be deposited but were advised that the money had not yet been transferred from the UK. As we had some time on our hands Rob and I wandered around Connaught Place, an area where the British Colonial influence was very much in evidence.

Connaught Place was named after Queen Victoria's third son, the Duke of Connaught who strangely enough had an oblique connection to our family. Thomas Hurdwell, our great grandfather had been working on the Duke's estate at Bagshot Park in 1895 as a forester when he was killed after the bough of a tree fell on him. It was then left to his eldest son, our grandfather, James Thomas Hurdwell, to provide for his mother and four younger siblings as no compensation was available to relatives of accident victims in those days.

The buildings in Connaught Place had been built in a semi circular fashion similar to the style of the Georgian Royal Crescent in Bath, England, with colonnades on the ground floor and residences on the upper storey. Within the open colonnades small retailers plied their trade selling various items to tourists and passers-by. Although there were many bargains to be had, particularly goods made from wood and ivory, we were unable to make any purchases as we could foresee trouble transporting them to Australia. However, I did buy a 14 carat gold nib 'Swan' fountain pen which is still in use almost fifty years later.

Following a light meal we returned to the Youth Hostel where we draped mosquito nets over our beds before retiring. Just as we were dozing off I started to experience severe abdominal pains. I had succumbed to what Europeans aptly described as the dreaded 'Delhi belly'. The pain was excruciating and my stomach felt as though it had been strangled into tightly constricted knots. I was dying to relieve myself but was not brave enough to venture out into the snake infested gardens. Instead I sat on the side of my bed rolled up in a ball pressing the cheeks of my backside together for what appeared to have been an eternity.

As the welcome dawn appeared I grasped the wooden staff and bashing it furiously upon the ground made my way to the open toilet. What a sublime relief! However I didn't feel like eating anything that day and decided to rest in bed for the remainder of the day.

We made an early start the next morning and drove straight to the Nepalese Embassy. Unfortunately the person we needed to see had been taken to the local hospital (probably suffering from Delhi belly) but we were advised that he would be back shortly. A couple of hours later we returned and true to their word our visas were ready for collection. We then called at the bank and were advised that the money from England could be collected the following day.

Having survived the privations of the youth hostel we were more than happy to leave. The facilities had been rudimentary to say the least but a less pleasing aspect had been the fact that sleeping on the ground floor balcony we had been troubled by some really weird noises emanating from the garden just minutes after the sun had set. Animals could be heard scurrying about and some were even howling and screaming, creating the impression that we were sharing the area with a skulk of jackals. This made sleep rather difficult to come by.

After parking the vehicles in Connaught Place, our first call was to the bank where we were greeted with some alarming news. We would only be able to take possession of our money (needed for the eventual purchase of airline tickets to Australia) if Geoff were present. This was a most unexpected development as we had no idea as to his present whereabouts or when he was likely to arrive at the bank.

Lyn immediately called at the American Express Offices where it was confirmed that Geoff, Anne and Brian had already picked up their mail and after a great deal of detective work on Lyn's part, she managed to locate them, thus enabling us all to attend the bank together and receive our money.

When we eventually returned to our vehicles we were confronted by some youths who claimed to have washed the Bedford. They were now demanding money for their efforts and from then on they followed us wherever went. By now we had become thoroughly fed up with being harassed by hawkers and salesmen demanding that we purchase their wares so it was decided that we should seek some peace by leaving Delhi behind us. Taking the road towards Agra we eventually found a camp site in a field. As it was still early evening this gave us the chance to inspect the broken spring on the Jeep.

It was now the 14th of October and we made an early start for the drive to Agra. We were aware that the broken spring on one side of the vehicle was placing a strain on the other springs and this made us proceed with greater care. However this didn't prevent our running over a two metre snake that still managed to slither away from the scene. Unfortunately luck was not on our side that morning as a leaf on the other rear spring also broke but after taking the Jeep to a mechanical workshop in Agra, two new leaves for the vehicle's springs were forged at a very moderate cost.

We were very much looking forward to having our first glimpse of the world's most celebrated building as we drove through a street in Agra with the Jeep's doors pinned back, excitedly speculating upon the forthcoming experience. Suddenly someone threw a large dollop of camel dung at the vehicle, hitting Jack fair and square in the right ear. He was naturally furious and I could hear him yelling "filthy bastards!" as he tried to shake the manure out of his ear. By the time we had stopped the vehicles to take our first view of the Taj some kilometres away he was still not in a suitable mood to appreciate the wondrous sight before him. However, he had simmered down considerably by the time we had parked the vehicles a couple of hundred metres from the Taj itself.

What a truly superb building. Certainly the most outstanding building we had ever seen. Breathtaking in its beauty! As there were few people around and no guards or fees required to view the building, we were able to make the most of our experience. We walked through the first arch and beheld the amazing tomb which had been completed in 1630 having taken 20,000 men over twenty years to construct. The Taj Mahal was set in expansive and immaculately kept gardens with a long pool leading up to the Seventh Wonder of the World. As we approached the building we were able to admire the mass of decorations fashioned from semi precious stones set into the pure white marble.

After removing our shoes we rushed into the actual tomb area as the marble beneath our feet was extremely hot. Inside we admired two replica tombs although the actual tombs themselves were in the basement with the duplicate tombs being housed above at ground level. We were somewhat startled when the guide let out an ear piercing yell to demonstrate how the sound carried throughout the whole building. The sound reverberated for a full fifteen seconds. The guide then showed us where the Ko-i-Noor Diamond had originally resided but which had been 'gifted' to the British during colonial days and is now incorporated in the Crown Jewels.

After leaving the Taj Mahal we cooked a meal before returning later that night to view the building in moonlight. We were completely alone. There were no guards or attendants. Unfortunately there was only a half moon but even so we could feel the vastness and majestic presence of the most famous building in the world.

After a final glimpse at the Taj Mahal we left Agra, eventually camping on the road to Kanpur.

The following morning we continued on our way to Kanpur but after a while were forced to stop at a section of road that had been submerged following recent flooding. No attempt had been made to make the road serviceable so we covered the vehicles' distributors with polythene bags and managed to navigate the next four hundred metres in water that was up to half a metre in depth.

After covering only one hundred and sixty kilometres that day we were still fifty kilometres short of Kanpur where we camped overnight. However we arrived there without further incident at 9.30 the next morning.

From what little we were able to see of the industrial capital of the state of Uttar Pradesh, Kanpur appeared to have been rather run down although one of its assets was that it had a railway station that linked the town to India's capital, New Delhi.

As we had taken a number of 8 mm movie films and 35mm still photographs of the Taj Mahal we were anxious to post them back to the U K. Accordingly we found a local post office, purchased the necessary postage stamps and placed the films in the mail. Sadly, none of these packages ever found their way to England. We later presumed that the stamps had been removed and sold again.

By evening we had journeyed to Allahabad, the city where Pundit Nehru's ashes had been scattered in the River Ganges some years before, but there found ourselves gridlocked in the thick of a huge crowd of locals celebrating some festival. Having become tired of crowded towns and their concomitant chaos, we found a detour that took us out of the centre of the town and to the relative peace of the surrounding countryside where we set up camp. Unfortunately it had now become apparent that wherever we chose to stop, local people would mysteriously appear from nowhere, squatting only a few metres from where we had camped. The more inquisitive bystanders even lifted lids from our saucepans in order to see what we were cooking. As darkness fell, the crowds around our camp site gradually drifted away until eventually the last spectators lost interest and left us in peace.

Needing fresh supplies we stopped early the following day at a small village on the way to Patna in order to purchase some potatoes and eggs. As we bundled the potatoes into a bag the woman serving us picked out all the smallest eggs. We ignored her choice and painstakingly selected the largest ones instead.

At lunch time we found a deserted area next to a rice paddy where we were able to enjoy our lunch in peace, free from crowds of curious onlookers. This gave us the chance to inspect the rice paddy where we made the interesting discovery that the channels between the rows of rice were not only inhabited by fish but also by frogs and small crayfish as well.

After another two hundred kilometres we managed to find a secluded spot in a wood where we camped for the night and were most agreeably surprised when, just after sunset, the trees came alive, having been illuminated by hundreds of fireflies.

As the dawn broke we found that our remote campsite had once again become a busy area as the usual agglomeration of inquisitive locals that had emerged to find out what we were doing, many of whom were spitting red betel nut juice or just expectorating only centimetres away from our cooking area. By staring out the worst offenders we managed to shift them to at least out of spitting range. Needless to say after we had packed up we were very relieved to enjoy the comparative solitude afforded whilst travelling in the vehicles.

When we eventually arrived in Patna we were disappointed to find that we were unable to board a vehicular ferry across the River Ganges, being obliged, instead to drive on towards Mokama Bridge. En route we watched in fascination as elephants lifted heavy logs onto trucks in a nearby wood. That night we made camp well after dark.

The next day, the 19th October we awoke to find a crowd of spitting locals around our camp but after a few staring sessions most of them retreated to a more comfortable distance. After driving all day we set up camp close to the Indian/Nepalese border. As we were unpacking our equipment a young Indian man who spoke impeccable English advised us that the Labour Party in Britain had just been elected and that Harold Wilson was now Prime Minister of Britain.

To continue towards the Nepalese border it was necessary to cross a small river where we expected to find a suitable bridge. However the old bridge had recently been demolished and the new bridge was yet to be completed. Our only means of crossing therefore was by way of an ancient wooden raft manned by just one ferryman. Getting our vehicles onto the old punt was nothing short of chaotic. Many ox carts were crowded onto the river bank and instead of forming an orderly queue before boarding the ferry they all rushed down to the landing stage cluttering the area so that nobody else was able access the vessel.

Eventually our two vehicles were loaded and the punt struggled towards the opposite bank without mishap. We made camp at Simra about five kilometres on the Indian side of the border.

NEPAL

Once again we awoke to find about fifty locals squatting nearby, spitting and generally getting in the way so we hastened to pack up as quickly as possible. By now we were very keen to be leaving India although having covered well over two thousand kilometres in that country it had been a most interesting experience culminating of course with our visit to the Taj Mahal. We would never be able to forget the splendour of that magnificent building.

With cheerful hearts we reached the border and, after paying the road toll and vehicle duty, we drove towards the foothills of the mighty Himalayas. We could hardly believe that we were now within reach of the exotic city of Kathmandu.

We remained in first gear as we drove upwards along a very steep narrow pass that wound its way around sheer cliff faces that overlooked rugged country on either side. At one point we stopped the vehicles and looked down upon the road we had just traversed where no less than twelve hairpin bends could be seen from our vantage point. The hillsides reminded us of those we had experienced in Norway although here we were able to see the occasional stall of banana trees dotted about these valleys.

Upon reaching an altitude of about three thousand metres we witnessed a crimson sunset flaming beneath the clouds. Having set up camp in these spectacularly picturesque surroundings we decided to enjoy an early night in order to soak up the peace and tranquillity of the surroundings, an experience we had sorely missed whilst travelling in India.

The 21st of October saw us out of our sleeping bags early only to find four Nepalese children nearby. We gave them some small presents including a few items of clothing that delighted them no end. Before resuming our drive Jerry and Rob poured some aviation fuel into the Bedford's petrol tank in order to enhance the Bedford's performance up the forthcoming steep gradients.

THE HIMALAYAS

It was a breathtaking experience to take our first glimpse of the mighty Himalayas still shrouded in white cloud cover. Peering over the side of the mountainous terrain we noticed that many small areas had been levelled into tiers on which crops were growing. People with whom we came into contact seemed animated and very friendly.

Following a very gruelling drive we finally arrived in Kathmandu in the early afternoon. Our first sight was that of two men at either end of a long pole under which was suspended a corpse wrapped in a white cloth. Presumably they were going to either a

cremation or a burial.

Shortly afterwards we got out of the vehicles and were straight away met by some youths who told us that we should get a good price for the vehicles. They also told us that if we wanted to fly out of Kathmandu the airlines would only accept hard currency and not the local Nepalese rupees. At the time we thought that the latter comment was rather strange.

Later on we were approached by several people who were interested in the Jeep but we decided that such matters would best be left for another time, besides the more pressing matter was to find accommodation. Eventually we settled on a room at the Hillview Hotel for the princely sum of one shilling and sixpence per night for the five of us.

For the first time in almost four months we were able to relax a little without being required to drive over horrendous roads encountering punctures and breakdowns on an almost daily basis. Also the break from driving gave the Jeep drivers the opportunity for their buttocks to have a rest after having endured thousands of kilometres perched on a thinly padded seat situated on the vehicle's petrol tank.

We took little time in depositing our belongings in our first floor room before wandering down the street to the Globe Cafe where we tucked into buffalo steak and vegetables for one shilling and three pence each.

Consequently we welcomed the prospect of staying in Kathmandu for some time during which we hoped to sell the Jeep and Bedford before travelling further south into Asia where we planned to board a plane in Singapore for our final destination of Sydney, Australia. In the meantime we would be able to soak up the atmosphere of this unique city of Kathmandu.

At one shilling and sixpence per night for the five of us, we did not expect the Hillview Hotel to exactly offer Five Star accommodation but at least it promised to provide a roof over our heads, not to mention a few unexpected surprises as well. The building was about fifty years old and very run down having been in need of a coat of paint for about the past three decades. Three single beds fitted snugly into our room, the beds consisting of frames over which strips of jute upholstery webbing had been fastened. A single latticed window that was also equipped with solid timber shutters overlooked the main street below.

Our first night in the hotel was not a pleasant one. We settled down well enough in our sleeping bags, Lyn and Jerry on one bed, Jack on another leaving Rob and me head-to-toe on the remaining bed. For four of us the task of getting sleep was a matter of some urgency before the rasping noise of Jack's snoring was able to get underway. No sooner had we turned out the light than other intruders entered the room. Rats! A whole platoon of them descended upon us, rushing around the floor and scratching around the cupboards looking for food. At one point I felt a rat at the end of my sleeping bag and pondered the fact that if it was perched on my foot it wouldn't have been very far from Rob's face either. On asking Rob if this was so he replied that he couldn't see one near his face but that he had one on the end of his sleeping bag.

Suddenly we heard a scream. A rat had found its way into Lyn's sleeping bag. We immediately switched on the light and the contingent of very large rats ran up the wall and out of the window. To the startled occupants of our room they appeared to have been the size of Shetland ponies.

We took little time in securing the wooden shutters and for a little while afterwards our newly found peace was sporadically shattered by the sound of furious rats barging the shutters in an effort to get back in again to finish their meals. The only redeeming factor of the night's events was that Jack had become so worried about the rats that it took him longer than the rest of us to get to sleep, thus enabling us to miss the sound of his sonorous snoring at least for a while.

Kathmandu, situated as it is within the largest valley in the world was a fascinating place in 1964. With its narrow streets and pagodas, not to mention cattle roaming everywhere, it gave the impression of an ancient village that had been frozen in time. There were hardly any vehicles on the streets and it appeared that most goods were transported on foot by heavily laden Sherpas. The sight of children smoking cigarettes was also very evident.

It didn't take long for us to ascertain that Kathmandu was a centre of intrigue. Wherever we went we came across travellers and locals whispering information about rates of exchange, airline fares, visas, motor vehicle sales and a host of other different topics.

Rates of exchange for Nepalese rupees into hard currency tended to vary on a daily basis depending upon supply and demand. In fact the town had become a microcosm of stock exchanges in the world outside.

On the first full day we got up early and cleaned the vehicles which engendered quite a lot of interest from some of the locals, in fact it elicited an offer of eight thousand Nepalese rupees (about eight hundred dollars) for the Jeep by a Mr Cherchard, a local Nepalese businessman. He had delegated finalization of the deal to his agent, an Indian by the name of Mr Giri. We were given five hundred rupees deposit on the spot with the promise of another three thousand in cash two days later plus a cheque for the balance a further day after that. It all sounded too good to be true. Buoyed by the sale of the Jeep Jerry and Rob were expecting to be able to sell the Bedford for considerably more.

In the evening we again visited the Globe Cafe for buffalo steaks that were very tough and required a great deal of chewing. Nevertheless they were quite tasty and doubtless possessed the necessary nutrients for which our bodies had been in need for some time, particularly as we had all lost about a quarter of our body weight.

In the midst of enjoying our steaks the quiet atmosphere of the cafe was suddenly shattered by a loud Australian voice shouting "What bum's swiped me jam?" Looking around we noticed a tall, dark haired Australian by the name of Ian Bersten. It transpired that overseas travellers who regularly frequented the Globe Cafe were in the habit of buying jars of jam and leaving them in a cabinet within the cafe itself. Following a meal at the Globe they would take their jam from the window cabinet and spread it on the bread previously purchased from a nearby bakery.

We took an instant liking to Ian who had been in Kathmandu for some time and next morning he gave us a guided tour of the town's lesser known haunts which proved to be most instructive to us newly arrived travellers. Months later when we had all finally settled down in Australia we kept in touch with Ian. He was later to become a well known entrepreneur, eventually starting a coffee importing company that became renowned throughout Australia.

The following day Jack and I received another three thousand rupees in cash from Mr Cherchard via Mr Giri plus a cheque for the balance to be cashed at the local bank a day later.

Thus after only a couple of days Jack and I were more than happy with the current situation and looked forward to cashing the remaining cheque and so finalising the transaction.

By then an Indian by the name of Gopal who marketed his soap as **Lifeduoy** and **Sunsight** (a corruptions of the English soaps, Lifebuoy and Sunlight) had become interested in the purchase of the Bedford van although from the outset Jerry and Rob had suspicions that he would be a very tricky character to deal with.

On the following day Jack went to the bank as planned but on presenting the cheque was told that the cheque required Mr Giri's endorsement in order to have it cashed. We smelt a rat and felt that someone at the bank must have been conspiring with Giri. When Jack approached Giri he still refused to endorse the cheque unless the amount was reduced, obviously a scheme to grab more money for himself. However, a day later I took the cheque to the bank and was paid the money in full. On the way back to the Hillview Hotel I saw Giri and rushed up to him and yelled out "You're a crook!"

Early next morning Giri came to see us in our hotel room and it soon became apparent that he was still unaware that the cheque had already been cashed. He told us that he would not endorse the cheque unless we were prepared to accept a reduced amount of money. I refused and told him that he hadn't been straight with us and pointing to the door I yelled "There's the door!" He looked somewhat nonplussed and replied "I know there is the door." We then told him to get out of the room. He was furious with me but we felt certain that his fury would soon be outmatched by his rage when he learned that the cheque had already been cashed and that his efforts at double dealing had failed.

On the following day whilst Jerry and Rob were out trying to sell the Bedford I decided to trek up to the Buddhist Temple overlooking Kathmandu. I was naturally very wary as I had about seven thousand rupees in my money belt. However I felt it would be safer on my person than leaving such a large sum at the hotel. I was also very careful to keep my eyes open should Giri have employed someone to follow me.

Up at the temple I took several movie shots of the monkeys that roamed around the temple gardens as well as shots of the temple itself. As my camera was not equipped with a zoom lens I tried to crawl up to one monkey to take a close up but it took exception to my presence and grabbed my hair. I was amazed at his strength and it took a considerable amount of time wrestling with the animal in order to extricate myself from its grip. In the meantime the monks were holding some sort of concert. The noise was absolutely frightful and sounded more like a Gerard Hoffnung Concert.

On my return journey I stopped by the banks of a river for a moment to watch two men tending a bonfire but after a while I spotted a human foot protruding from the smouldering embers. It was apparently a cremation and as firewood was in short supply the body had been folded over during the cremation process.

The night of the 30th October afforded us very little sleep due to a multitude of circumstances. Jack managed to rev up his snores a couple of notches in spite of having various articles thrown at him during the night. The Indian truck drivers in the next room kicked up a terrible din and having finally drifted off to sleep their snoring attained an even higher decibel rating than Jack's. Rats fought to get into the room, fleas bit us and mosquitoes bombarded us throughout the night.

Whilst all this was going on some English travellers who had been locked out of the hotel tried to gain access by throwing articles at the windows. This last annoyance was too much for us so we emptied mugs of water over them. Thinking that it was urine they left in a hurry.

Rats were a constant problem and any items of food had to be either carried with us throughout the day or be firmly locked away. During our time in Kathmandu we met a very likeable but rather pukka Englishman who had been educated at a select British public school. This charming fellow had two possessions that he treasured above all else. One was a large piece of cheese purchased from the local dairy at considerable expense and the other was his brown Harris Tweed jacket. As he was wary of either item being stolen he used to wrap the cheese in greaseproof paper which he then covered in newspaper before wrapping his Harris Tweed jacket around the whole lot before placing it under his pillow at night.

We met him at the Globe one morning and he was crestfallen as he held up his tweed jacket displaying a large hole in its back. Apparently whilst he was asleep rats had gnawed their way through his jacket and the newspaper until they were able to make off with his treasured chunk of cheese.

On the final day of October with the objective of viewing Mount Everest, Jerry, Rob and I took the

Bedford along the road to Nagacot as far as we were able to drive before parking and continuing our journey on foot. We walked through tiny villages where rice was being harvested and threshed by women with babies strapped to their backs. The going was quite difficult in parts and on many occasions we were compelled to deviate onto Sherpa tracks. Having reached our ultimate goal of an elevated vantage point we were very disappointed by the cloud cover that denied us our view of the famous peak. However, a little later the cloud lifted and we were able to catch a glimpse of the mighty Mount Everest on top of the world.

The first day of the new month seemed to augur well for the sale of the Bedford as Mr Gopal (the soap maker) offered a firm price of five thousand rupees for the vehicle.

Jack and Lyn had returned from a flying trip to the Pokhara Valley so we all celebrated at the Globe over an evening meal. By now Jack had decided that he wanted to leave Kathmandu and had booked a flight to Dhaka in East Pakistan (later to become Bangladesh) leaving the following day. He planned to leave details of his travel plans at the American Express offices in Dhaka and Bangkok which would enable us to rendezvous with him later.

However, Gopal, the prospective purchaser of the Bedford, having seen one of our number leave surmised that we would all be in a hurry to leave as well and so reneged on the previously agreed price of five thousand rupees, reducing his offer by one thousand rupees. Jerry and Rob told him what he could do with his rupees and cancelled the deal.

By now there were just the four of us and we had become heartily sick of the Hillview Hotel, especially the rats and fleas. We therefore decided to camp in the open air on the perimeter of land owned by the local Kathmandu Hospital. In the meantime Jerry and Rob wrote a note to Mr Cherchard (the purchaser of the Jeep) asking if he would be interested in buying the Bedford.

Next day we were awoken by Mr Cherchard who was making some enquiries about Giri. When we told him about Giri and his double dealing over the Jeep, Mr Cherchard became extremely annoyed. Unbeknown to us at that time, Giri had disappeared.

Mr Cherchard told us that he was interested in the Bedford and that he would let us know his offer shortly. True to his word he sent his driver round in the afternoon to say that he would offer five thousand rupees but that the vendors would have to pay the customs duty. The offer was refused.

By now it had become apparent that it would be some time before the Bedford could be sold and after some discussion it was decided that Lyn and I should travel to East Pakistan and then on to Bangkok where we would eventually link up with Jack and then wait for Jerry and Rob after they had disposed of the Bedford.

Heavily laden and carrying as much hand luggage as possible we hoisted it into the Bedford which promptly ran out of petrol before we had hardly moved. Fortunately a friend took us to the airline office in stages on his motor bike getting us there just before the bus was due to leave for Kathmandu airport.

Thick fog delayed our departure for one and a half hours but finally the old DC3 cleared the runway and we were airborne. We were very sorry that Rob and Jerry were not with us as we had been looking forward so much to leaving together.

EAST PAKISTAN

On arrival at Dhaka Airport the plane door opened and as we walked across the tarmac we almost fried in the midday heat. Because the weight of our main luggage was limited to forty pounds per person we had dressed in our heaviest items of clothing before boarding the plane and were now paying the penalty by almost dissolving in the hot Dhaka sun. Still sweating profusely and encumbered by so many items of awkward luggage we hired a scooter rickshaw and instructed the driver to take us to the local railway station. At the station we suddenly realised that we had not as yet changed our money into Pakistani rupees. However while we were explaining our problem to the rickshaw driver a local gentleman observed our predicament, paid the rickshaw driver then dumped our luggage into the boot of his car. He then took us to his home where we deposited our bags before being taken to the Pakistan International Airways Office to enquire about our onward journey to Thailand including whether we required Thai visas.

We were very appreciative of Mr Tufal's hospitality and were only too happy to accept his invitation to accompany him to an international soccer match between Ceylon (now Sri Lanka) and Pakistan that afternoon. Naturally we cheered for the home team which won. Later on we ended the day at a Chinese restaurant for dinner.

The following day I again made some enquiries about our Thai visas and was told that Calcutta was probably the nearest place where they could be obtained. We needed photographs for our visas so Mr Tufal kindly suggested that we borrow his new Hillman Imp car in which to make a few calls in Dhaka. We also combined our outing with some sightseeing as well.

After returning to Mr Tufal's home I started to feel quite unwell and thought that I was developing a cold but after a couple of Aspros and a good sleep I felt a lot better and was able to join Lyn and Mr Tufal for an evening drink where we were introduced to an ex-army Major, a politician and Jimmy, the director of an international travel agency. The company was very pleasant with excellent surroundings to match. Major Naushad Ali Khan gave us the address of his club in Chittagong and insisted we call on him when in that city.

Lyn and I got on very well with Mr Tufal who suggested that we go for a drive in the morning and meet up with Jimmy later on. The countryside was lush and green with several lakes on which sampans drifted along often obscured behind palm trees on the shoreline. Jimmy proved to be a most personable character and possessed a keen sense of humour. He had lived in London for two years and counted among his friends, personalities such as Bruce Forsyth, Acker Bilk and the Queen's fashion designer, Norman Hartnell.

Following a meal at Jimmy's house we drove to the railway station where we purchased tickets for the journey to Chittagong. The railway station was crowded and as our train was due to leave at any moment we had difficulty pushing our way through the throng of travellers to reach our carriage.

Our seats were in the 'inter class' compartment, this being one class lower than first class. We sat on benches facing passengers on the opposite side of the carriage. An hour later the old steam train chugged its way out of Chittagong station, by which time we had become accepted by the other passengers who were keen to chat to us, offering us fruit, tea and sweets. One gentleman dressed in a long cotton cape told us that his son was studying law in London. He seemed very refined although we were somewhat taken aback when he lifted his long cotton gown, scratched his bum and emitted a loud fart. Making ourselves comfortable on the floor of the carriage we slept soundly surrounded by these very kind and friendly people.

At Chittagong we found the station's First Class exit and for ten rupees a night booked a room in the First Class Rest Room before contacting Mr Farouk on Jimmy's recommendation. Mr Farouk had been expecting us and insisted on taking us to the offices of Pakistan International Airways in order to confirm whether we required visas in order to stay in Thailand. PIA confirmed that we did require visas and arrangements were made for me to fly to Calcutta for that purpose.

Later on we went to lunch with Mr Farouk and in the evening had a relaxed walk along a beach where a little orphaned boy, no more than six years of age showed us around by the light of a lantern. After dinner Lyn and I returned to our room at the railway station commenting on how unbelievably kind and hospitable the people of both West and East Pakistan had been.

Lyn and I got up early the following day, packed up our few belongings and moved to a very cheap boarding house called the Gulistan Hotel for Men. It was not the most salubrious place in which to stay but we thought it would suit our needs and our pockets for a few days although in retrospect it would have rivalled many of the oldest buildings in London's pre war slums.

Once again, we met Mr Farouk who suggested that we drive down to 'the longest beach in the world' at Cox's Bazaar. The drive proved to be very interesting as the pattern of the landscape on either side of the road appeared to change the further our journey progressed; there were rice paddies, banana trees, teak and rubber tree plantations, thick forests and eventually jungle.

What we saw of Cox's Bazaar was not quite as impressive as we had been led to believe although we obviously hadn't the time to survey the whole seventy miles of beach. However we did see some rather impressive bright red crabs with huge white eyes scurrying across the sand in front of us.

We returned to Chittagong in time to share a meal and a bottle of gin with our host before making our way back to the Gulistan where we spent a terrible night. It was a humid, steamy night and our discomfort was heightened by the breakdown of the fan in our room. The mosquito nets were peppered with holes, their only function appearing to have been in trapping the bed bugs. The person in the next room cleared his throat incessantly, making a revolting noise in the process.

Next day was the 11th of November and time for me to fly to Calcutta. I boarded a Pakistan International Airways Fokker Friendship plane where a chance in a million occurred. The person sitting next to me was Gordon Sade, an English Baptist Church Missionary who knew Frank Houten, a person whom I had previously known in England. He took me to the Calcutta Missionary HQ where I briefly met up with Frank again. Later on Mr Sade took me to the Red Shield Club where I stayed the night for seven rupees.

My stay at the Club was quite interesting. An Indian traveller to whom I had spoken that evening was sharing my dormitory and during the night he decided to relieve himself. Instead of going to the designated toilets he urinated from our dormitory doorway into the adjoining dining area and then got back into bed. Next morning fearing that the dining room staff might have thought that I had been the culprit, I delayed my entrance into the dining room until within earshot of a member of the staff I mentioned my sense of disgust at such an occurrence.

The Thai Embassy was on a tram route so, armed with the necessary directions I made my way to the nearest tram stop. Getting onto a tram turned out to be quite an unusual experience as none of the trams actually stopped but merely slowed down at which time several travellers alighted as others struggled to get on. After three trams had followed the same procedure I enquired of a gentleman next to me why the trams always failed to stop. He replied "If they stopped, Sahib, everyone would get on!"

When I arrived at Thai the embassy there was a sign on the door advising that there was a twenty-four hour wait for visas, however, they were very co-operative and had them ready by early afternoon.

I liked Calcutta although I found it to have been such a sprawling city with no well defined quarters for embassies or airline offices. This wasn't very convenient as far as I was concerned. However the people were very friendly, far friendlier than the locals we had met in Delhi and those who spoke English went out of their way to be helpful.

I was very impressed with the Victoria Memorial which reminded me of some areas in London although, of course, Calcutta had been the second city of Queen Victoria's British Empire and was referred to by her as the 'Jewel in the Crown'. Wherever I went there were hand drawn rickshaws transporting the more opulent members of society around and I felt extremely sorry for the poor men consigned to a life of such subservience as they trudged the streets barefoot hauling their loads of human cargo behind them.

I caught the afternoon flight back to Chittagong via Dacca and was surprised to bump into Mr Tufal at Dacca Airport. I thanked him again for his generosity and for introducing us to some of his friends.

Having arrived back at the Gulistan with the visas Lyn and I chatted before bed bug hunting and an indifferent night's sleep.

On the following day after posting some mail we were taking a walk when we bumped into Major Naushad Ali Khan who invited us to the Chittagong Club. As it was a Friday and a Muslim dry day, we sat in his room chatting, he smoking Dutch cigars whilst Lyn and I had a couple of drinks. He was delightful company. He told us of his army experiences, about local customs and Pakistan's local politics since separation from India in 1947. He spoke of arranged marriages and told us that he had met his wife only three times before their wedding but did assure us that their arranged marriage had worked well for them as they both had been able to start out on the path of matrimony as fresh travellers.

He also told us that in Pakistan family feuds led to hundreds of murders each year in the name of family honour. Apparently it was not unusual for a man in the twentieth century to be murdered because a person belonging to another family had been killed several generations before. After arranging to meet him at the club the following night we returned to the Gulistan in the rain.

The next afternoon we called in on Mr Farouq to say goodbye and to thank him for all he had done for us. His help had been much appreciated. In the early evening we took our baggage to the PIA Offices for them to look after until our flight the next day. The staff entertained us with drinks of Coca Cola and cakes before we parted, bound for the Chittagong Club.

We then spent a very enjoyable evening with Major Naushad Ali Khan which was rounded off with supper at 3 am. As Lyn was very tired the Major insisted that Lyn sleep on his bed under the fan and mosquito net whilst he and I chatted until 6 a.m. whereupon Lyn and I departed for the PIA flight bound for Bangkok.

BURMA

For some reason our flight did not go straight to Bangkok but touched down at Burma's capital, Rangoon. We were told that we would not be departing for Bangkok until the next day but in the meantime were to be put up at the Grand Palace Hotel in Rangoon at Pakistan International Airline's expense.

It seemed strange being ushered into the foyer of this palatial hotel carrying our battered old rucksacks. This certainly marked a stark contrast to our arrival at the flee-ridden Gulistan Hotel for Men in Chittagong. The commodious room allotted to us with its marble floors and high ceilings, was the last word in luxury.

As it was early afternoon we decided to go for a walk around Rangoon, our first destination being the famous Shwedagon Pagoda. This building's massive golden dome dominated the buildings around it and at a height of ninety-nine metres was almost as tall as the dome of London's St Pauls Cathedral. Walking up the steps to the pagoda we were approached by a guide who offered to show us around for a fee of eight shillings. After settling for a lower sum we removed our shoes at the entrance and walked inside. Within the quiet atmosphere of the dome we spent some time looking at the great golden Buddha whilst still marvelling at the beauty and sheer size of the dome.

Although we spent very little time in Rangoon it seemed to us to have been a city of strange contradictions. Whilst it appeared to have been quite modern in terms of its layout there were very few items of merchandise in the shops, a similar situation to that which one would have expected to find in Communist countries at that time.

In the evening we enjoyed a most superb meal in the Grand Palace Hotel's dining room before retiring to our well appointed room. I thoroughly enjoyed the luxury of slipping into the en suite bath and letting the warm foamy suds lap over my body before hopping out onto its beautiful marble floor - all paid for by PIA.

We were called at 4.30 the next morning and received breakfast a few minutes later. The United Burma Airways flight to Bangkok was made in a Vickers Viscount prop jet plane that was exceptionally comfortable with plenty of leg room. The in-flight service was also excellent. We even enjoyed another breakfast whilst in flight.

THAILAND

Driving from the Airport in a Mercedes taxi our first impression was that Bangkok was an extremely Americanized city with wide roads and modern motor cars. However we soon found that the areas away from the city had managed to retain their original Siamese atmosphere with palm trees and small shops that appeared to sell everything from items such as gold and silver jewellery to clothing made from Thai silk.

Included in our mail at the American Express Office was a note from Jack telling us that he was staying at the local Youth Hostel. We therefore made our way there and found Jack who was very pleased to see Lyn and me although surprised that Jerry and Rob were not with us.

Next day we had breakfast at a dining hall in a nearby school after which the three of us wandered around the local shopping area situated on the banks of a nearby klong. We were very much taken by the people who were helpful and very friendly. Returning to the Youth Hostel we met Mike, an Aussie whom I had previously met in Calcutta who told us that Jerry was in hospital in Calcutta after collapsing at the Thai Embassy with severe stomach pains. Apparently Rob was staying nearby at the Offices of Burmese Airways whilst awaiting Jerry's recovery. We were extremely worried and were hopeful that he would be able to join us shortly.

We all loved Bangkok and were lucky enough to have been there during the annual Moon Festival where there was an air of gaiety about the city with masses of people everywhere. In the evening we stood on the banks of the river and saw people floating small paper boats in which they had placed lighted candles. It was quite a novel sight to see myriad little craft dancing on the water as they drifted downstream.

One morning we rose very early and caught a bus into town where a few of us hired a motor launch that took us to the famous floating markets. The launch slowly made its way along the klongs where nearby palm trees on either bank were reflected in the brownish water. Small house boats were dotted about the shores and it was interesting to see children, some in school uniform, preparing to go to school in tiny dinghies. Sampans were plying to and fro selling fruit and vegetables whilst other craft sold coffee and other refreshments. On the banks of the klongs, shops situated on timber stilts were selling silks, wood carvings and items of cheap jewellery.

Our cruise ended with a visit to the Temple of Dawn before we eventually returned to the hostel three hours later.

To our great relief the following day we were reunited with Jerry and Rob who had just flown in from Calcutta. Jack, Lyn and I couldn't wait to hear about their difficulties after we had left them in Kathmandu.

Having told Gopal that he was a scheming shyster they then redoubled their efforts to sell the Bedford in order to leave Kathmandu and join the rest of the crew. Fortunately they came across a Canadian Missionary working as a mechanic for a Christian organisation who wanted to purchase the van. He inspected the vehicle and offered them one hundred British pounds, twice the amount that they had originally paid for the vehicle back in England. As they were keen to have the money in British pounds he gave them a cheque which was to be cashed outside Nepal. They were obviously taking a chance but they felt that he was an honourable person and accepted the cheque. Happily they were able to cash it on arrival in Singapore.

Jerry and Rob flew out of Kathmandu to Patna in India in the same rickety DC3 that Lyn and I had used and it appeared that the pilot navigated by following the road below. From Patna they took a very overcrowded train to Calcutta and went straight to the United Burma Airways Office in the Central Business District. Here they booked their flight to Bangkok via Rangoon. Upon requesting where to find the cheapest accommodation they were surprised to be told that they could sleep in the Airways office after the close of business. They were also advised that they were required to obtain visas for Thailand.

Having lodged their application for visas, they were in the waiting room of the Thai Embassy when Jerry suddenly became very ill and collapsed clutching his stomach. Needless to say Rob became very alarmed and sought urgent help from the office staff who initially thought that the condition was not serious but was probably 'Delhi belly'. However as his condition rapidly deteriorated he was taken to a private hospital which, mercifully, was situated next door. Once it was confirmed that they had a health insurance policy they treated Jerry for kidney stones and kept him in hospital overnight.

That evening Rob, not without some trepidation, went back to the UBA building wondering what sort of reception he would receive when he sought a bed for the night. As previously instructed he knocked on the back door of the office building and was received by the caretaker, a magnificent Sikh with a bushy beard and immaculate white turban. Sure enough, Rob was invited to take his pick of where to sleep and chose a long desk where the phones and office paraphernalia had been removed. He slept soundly.

The next day Rob visited Jerry in hospital and was relieved to find him much improved. The Doctor suggested that Jerry stay there another night and Rob eventually returned that evening to his 'accommodation' at the Airline Office. This time, upon entering the office he found it full of Burmese people who apparently were being expelled as illegal immigrants. Rob spent a sleepless night unsure as to the integrity of his fellow travellers. Fortunately his apprehensions proved to be unfounded.

Next day Jerry was released from hospital allowing them both to travel to Bangkok via Rangoon. Their experience on the flight to Bangkok was similar to that which Lyn and I had undergone a couple of weeks before in the Vickers Viscount plane. After touching down in Rangoon they were told that their plane was not scheduled to fly to Bangkok until the next day.

Thus, they were escorted to the rather classy 'Trafalgar Hotel' where they were to spend the night. Whilst at dinner that evening they met an interesting person who was the head of the 'Bahai' faith in Australia. Upon seeing Jerry and Rob and noticing that they were all skin and bone, he called the waiter over and gave him instructions to let them start at the beginning of the menu and allow them to keep going until they were full.

The next day they left Rangoon bound for Bangkok where they were reunited with the rest of the family.

Unfortunately Jerry and Rob's stay in Bangkok lasted only a few days although during that time the five of us did manage to visit some very interesting places. This included the local snake farm where we were able to see a variety of venomous snakes including the dreaded cobras and king cobra.

At the farm we were told that the manufacture of anti venin involved injecting horses with snake venom which then caused the horse's immune system to generate an antidote from which they manufactured the anti venin. I did feel very sorry for the two horses that we saw at the snake farm.

By now it was the 23rd November and all of us were keen to move on to Singapore. We therefore left the youth hostel and checked into a small hotel near to the Bangkok Railway Station where we booked rail tickets to Singapore. We also booked airline tickets from Singapore to Sydney aboard a BOAC (British Overseas Airways Corporation) flight.

Two days later we caught the 4.15 pm train to Singapore which included a stopover in Penang in Malaysia. Twenty-seven hours later we arrived in Penang where we left the train and after an excellent meal at a small local cafe we took the ferry across to Penang Island where we booked into a small and inexpensive hotel for three shillings and sixpence per night.

We thoroughly enjoyed our stay on the island the highlight of which was a ride on the cable tramway up to the very top of Penang Hill. Our vantage point commanded a wonderful view of the island with its panoramic scenery that included tall palm trees as far as the eye could see.

In the evening we caught the return ferry to the mainland where we spent the night.

The train journey to Singapore was very tedious although whilst travelling through Malaysia we were most interested to see rubber trees with cups attached to their trunks designed to catch the latex.

As we were not occupying 'sleeper' carriages we made ourselves as comfortable as possible with some travellers stretching out across two seats whilst others spread their sleeping bags on the carriage floor.

After we had spent a rather restless night, the train stopped to allow railway staff to board in order to clean out the carriages. However, without warning the cleaners started to hose out the carriages catching many passengers unawares as they slept on the floor. Unfortunately Rob was one such unlucky person who became a victim at the hands of the somewhat overzealous cleaners.

We finally reached Singapore where we were very happy to leave the train and make for a fairly small but comfortable hotel at the cost of five shillings per person per night.

Whilst the others were settling in I went for a walk with Mike to 'Change Alley' where bargains were said to be had if looking for watches or radios. I purchased a small AIWA portable radio for three pounds.

In 1964 Singapore was very much as I had expected it to have been having read a lot about that city's troubles during the dark days of the Second World War when it fell to the Japanese. It appeared to have changed little since that time. Fortunately the brutal Japanese occupation was brought to an end after Japan's defeat by the Allies only nineteen years prior to our visit. Many of the streets were narrow with alleyways heading off in different directions, often leading to open markets and pavement cafes. It was interesting to see Raffles Hotel and Tea Rooms having read about it in countless travel magazines.

That night we all went to bed quite late but at 3 am were awoken by Lyn phoning for an ambulance for Jerry. He had again been taken ill with another kidney stone and was in tremendous pain, lying on his bed groaning in agony. The hotel management was very helpful and an ambulance quickly arrived to take Jerry to a nearby hospital. We all stayed up until we had been assured that he had been given pain killers and was sleeping peacefully.

Rob, Lyn and Jack postponed their flights to Sydney. However I confirmed my flight although I was advised that I would have to fly Air India via Perth and not direct to Sydney on a BOAC plane as I'd previously arranged.

On the last day of November, 1964 I boarded an Air India Boeing 707 for the flight to Perth. The weather during the flight was quite rough in parts with a lot of turbulence and lightning in fact the person sitting next to me in the window seat asked if I would mind changing seats as she didn't like looking at the lightning outside. I was only too happy to oblige. During the flight I was looking forward to a good meal but was very disappointed when yet another dollop of rice was served.

Part Six
AUSTRALIA

On the 1st of December, 1964 at 3 am my plane touched down in Perth, Western Australia. Although it was very early morning I found the Customs and Immigration people to be very friendly as I handed over the immigration papers I had been given to fill in on the Air India flight. "Why did you fill out these forms?" I was asked.

When I told the Customs Officer that they had been given to me on the plane he ceremoniously tore them up, tossed the pieces of paper into the air and said "If you're from England, you're one of us!" He then asked if I had anything I wished to declare and having replied in the negative he then asked if I had any knives with a blade over four inches long in my luggage. I told him that I had a couple of Ghurkha knives purchased in Nepal which I was then asked to produce. These knives were really evil looking things with sharp curved blades that in many ways looked very much like sharpened steel boomerangs. Having inspected them he said "They're fancy letter openers aren't they?" and let me put them back in my bag.

As I had nowhere to go and no hotel booked I asked if I could sleep in the airport waiting room. I stretched out on a couple of chairs and dozed off. It was a strange feeling for when I awoke from time to time I found that I had been left entirely on my own in the passenger lounge and didn't see a soul all night. It felt as though the airport had been closed for business and that I had been left as its sole occupant.

The airport cafe opened quite early and having had a look around the terminal first I joined the other cafe patrons and sat down waiting to be served. Eventually a waitress came up to my table and said "Are you right?" I was unable to understand her because I hadn't actually said anything and therefore I could not have been either right or wrong. Seeing the questioning look on my face she said "Have you ordered yet?" It was wonderful tucking into my first Australian breakfast of bacon and eggs.

I had quite a long time to wait before boarding my scheduled flight to Sydney so I walked out of the small terminal and into fields nearby where I sat under a gum tree listening to the unfamiliar sound of Australian birdlife for the very first time. Being on my own I felt a little lonely yet also filled with a feeling of quiet anticipation.

Just after midday I boarded an Ansett Boeing 727 jet and was lucky enough to find a number of Royal Australian Navy sailors on board who were bound for Adelaide. They were a very jovial lot and upon learning that this was my very first day in Australia were keen to tell me all about the country which made me feel very welcome as we chatted over the odd beer or three.

As the plane had a two hours refuelling stop in Adelaide I tried to ring an old friend I had met during my two years National service in the Royal Army Ordnance Corps back in 1955. Jock Barnes had left his home in Edinburgh some years before and had migrated to Adelaide. Unfortunately there was no reply.

The flight from Adelaide to Sydney took only ninety minutes and as we lost altitude I was able to catch my first glimpse of the lights of Sydney's outer suburbs below and wondered what life would have in store for me down there. We touched down at 8 pm and following Jerry's instructions I caught a cab to the suburban railway station of Rockdale where I purchased a ticket for the southern beachside suburb of Cronulla.

As Australia was a new country by comparison to ancient England I expected the train to have been a sparkling new model and was amazed when what was known as a 'red rattler' of 1920's vintage clanged its way into the station.

Less than half an hour later the train came to a stop at Cronulla during a downpour. Seeing a taxi I directed him to Arthur Street, Cronulla and having arrived at my destination he told me that the fare was "two and a tray". I had no idea what a tray was so I gave him three shillings. (I later found out that a tray was the Aussie slang word for three pence)

As they welcomed me into their home Lyn's parents were very surprised to see one lone traveller on their doorstep instead of five but they were much relieved when I told them that the others would follow shortly. After a very long chat it was great to go to bed in a private house. The journey in elderly vehicles had taken almost six months to complete but finally I was here on the opposite side of the globe.

A couple of days later Jerry, Lyn, Rob and Jack arrived, much to the satisfaction of Lyn's parents who hadn't seen their daughter or son-in-law for over two years.

HOLIDAY MAKER OR MIGRANT ?

Our first few days in Australia were spent meeting Lyn and Jerry's friends and attending barbecues at their homes.

We had all lost a lot of weight during our long journey, none more so than me who managed to tip the scales at just over fifty kilos (120 Pounds). The locals felt that we were in urgent need of good food and plenty of it. At that time the price of meat in Australia was a mere fraction of what we had been used to in England and in an endeavour to build us up we were served huge steaks that inevitably overlapped the sides of the large dinner plates on which they were served. I for one was unequal to the task of consuming such large quantities of carnivorous fare.

We sampled the charm of some of Sydney's magnificent beaches with sands that stretched for miles and the sight of the surf seemed to fulfil the images we had previously conjured up in our minds whilst rugged up at home in England during the winter twelve months before.

But above all we noticed the easy going nature of the people that we met which stood in stark contrast to the British reserve to which we had previously been accustomed. One example of this aspect of Australian familiarity occurred when Rob and I decided to attend the offices of the local Commonwealth Employment Service in Caringbah, a suburb about three kilometres from where we were staying in Cronulla.

The day was very hot but being British we felt that to obtain employment we would need to look smart and well groomed. Dressed in our heavy English worsted suits it was not long before we were sweating profusely as we walked to the employment exchange. By the time we had arrived at the offices we were dripping with perspiration.

It was quite a relief upon arrival at the employment office to relax in air conditioned comfort. As we filled in the necessary forms about our education and previous employment details we became aware, and not a little surprised to find that nobody else was wearing suits or ties in fact for the most part the other job seekers were neatly dressed in slacks and open neck shirts. Some even wore shorts.

Shortly afterwards I was invited into an office where the employment officer introduced himself before starting to read the form I had just completed. Having done so he then asked what sort of work I was looking for. I told him that having only just arrived in the country I would be happy to work in any clerical situation that was available. He then asked me if I would consider employment as a stock control clerk at an engineering company that hired out scaffolding and other building materials. He told me that the company was situated near to a railway station at St. Peters, a suburb only a fifteen kilometres from where I was currently living.

I told him that such a situation would suit me very well whereupon he picked up the phone and contacted a Mr Ed Skelton, the branch manager of that company. Sitting opposite the employment officer I became amazed at the conversation. "G'day Ed, I've got this Pommy bloke here just out from England who's looking for a job and I reckon that the stock control job would suit him pretty well. Looking through his application form I see that he's got a Diploma in Sociology from London University. Mate, he'll piss it in!"

Having established that the salary was eleven hundred pounds a year which was fine by me, he put the phone down and said "You've got the job – you start next Thursday". Naturally I imagined that the interview for the job was for that date but he assured me that I had actually secured the job without the need for an interview saying "No, mate, you've got the job, just report to Ed on Thursday at 8.30".

I felt so much at home in this casual 'no frills' environment that it was little wonder that I would not see England again for another eight years, and that was for a holiday.

Glossary

Bathing Machine	Covered shelter used in 19th century England for protecting female bathers' modesty whilst taking to the water.
Beau Brummel	Fashionable person in Regency England
Beau Geste	Soldier fighting in the French Foreign Legion
Billy	Australian iron pot mainly used for brewing tea over an open fire
British Public School	Despite its confusing title – a prestigious school for the children of so called upper class families
Butlin's Holiday Camp	Family Holiday Resort popular in Britain in the late twentieth century
Chatty	Earthenware pitcher for the storage of water.
Dorman Long	British Civil Engineering Company
G.I	Soldier in the US Armed forces
Klong	Thai Canal
Lilo	Brand of inflatable mattress
Pukka	British expression for 'correct in behaviour'
Punkah Wallah	Person in charge of operating a manual fan
Qanat	Fresh water fed from higher elevations in Iran and distributed to locations via a network of smaller canals
Welch Plug	Steel plug to be found in the cylinder block of a motor vehicle.

Acknowledgements

I wish to thank Alan Jones for regularly reading proofs of this narrative and offering suggestions along the way. His input was invaluable

He also 'cleaned up' many 35mm photographic slides that had been languishing in a cupboard for almost fifty years.

I would also wish to thank Wendy, my wife, for sorting out the many photos in readiness for inclusion within the pages of 'Overland on a Shoestring'.

BY THE SAME AUTHOR

SIRENS AND GREY BALLOONS

TRACTOR THE AUSTRALIAN WONDER CAT

Overland On A Shoestring Photos

1. RYF Willy's Jeep
2. LVW Willy's Jeep
3. Ready to Roll 29th June 1964
4. Bedford being loaded onto the good ship Venus at Newcastle.
5. Shanty homes in Naples
6. Orphaned kitten in Italy
7. Enjoying a beer with the Aitelikon Postmaster
8. Turkish mud hut village
9. Camp in the Iranian Desert
10. Camels refuelling in Iran
11. Author with fresh Iranian bread
12. Esfahan, Iran
13. Desert sandstorm brewing in Iran
14. Lyn and Jerry with the Bedford
15. Jack, Lyn, Jerry and Rob in Quetta, West Pakistan
16. Shalimar Gardens in Lahore, West Pakistan
17. Flooded Grand Trunk Road in India
18. Typical Indian village
19. The Taj Mahal in 1964
20. Awaiting punt ferry on Indian Nepalese border.
21. Foothills of the Himalayas
22. Nepalese children
23. Singapore Harbour in 1964
24. Perth International Airport in 1964.